DEATH SMELLS A ROSE

A PENELOPE STANDING MYSTERY

TESS BAYTREE

SPECULATIVE TURTLE PRESS

CHAPTER 1

$\mathcal{P}$enelope stopped walking, eyeing the path in front of her. A fragrant cedar branch larger than her body blocked the path up to the door of the Johnson house. Since there weren't any downed power lines in the area, she executed a slightly irregular grand jeté over the greenery. Her mailbag banged into her hip when she landed, but she still gave her leap a nine out of ten. Not bad. Her ballet technique was just as good in her fifties as it had been when she'd last taken lessons as a clumsy eight-year-old. With a graceful flourish of her hands, she shoved the advertising circulars through the mail slot.

Delivering mail the morning after a big wind storm let her find out about all the damage without feeling obligated to help clean it up. Mostly there were smaller branches littering the streets, and old fences knocked over, but a massive old oak a few streets away had gone down overnight. Luckily it had fallen away from the house, so nobody was hurt, but it had destroyed three cars. She could hear the chainsaws and a wood chipper from where she stood.

Penelope grabbed the next handful of mail, jumped back over the branch, and headed across the lawn to the next house. By evening, the entire town would be cleaned up, and the only evidence of the storm would be a few missing trees, some fresh wood chips, and all the posters for missing dogs that had cropped up on telephone poles this morning.

The annual Rose Garden Society Festival was just around the corner, and nobody was going to let a little thing like a wind storm get in the way of the perfect yard.

Halfway to the next house, a high-pitched bark from under a parked truck made Penelope stop. She crouched down to look and found a bedraggled Yorkshire terrier facing her. "Hello there." This wasn't one of the dogs on any of the posters she'd seen, but someone would be missing him. The mail could wait a few minutes.

Ten minutes and three treats later, Penelope had a wiggling Yorkie licking her face. She felt along the dog's pink collar for a tag. "Let's see if you have an address." A telephone number would be almost as good.

But the only information she got from the heart-shaped tag was the dog's name. Penelope had never understood that practice, though half her clients did the same thing. "Purdue, hm? We need to talk to your people about putting something useful on your tags."

Luckily, behind the name tag was the metal county license. Penelope couldn't read it with the dog in her arms — she still hadn't bought reading glasses because she couldn't possibly be old enough to need them — but the camera on her phone was just as good. One photo, a quick swipe with her fingers to enlarge the image, and she had the numbers on the tag. "Ha, we're cooking with gas now, Perdue. We have your serial number." She called animal services and only familiarity with the system kept her from panicking when the dispatcher answered.

"Nine one one, what's the nature of your emergency."

Penelope recognized the dispatcher's voice. "Hey, Rochelle. It's Penelope Standing. This isn't an emergency, so if you need to put me on hold, that's okay."

"Oh, hey Penelope! Nope, you're the only caller I've got at the moment. What's up?" She paused, then added. "You didn't find another body, did you?"

"No. At least, not yet." The question was a little unfair. It had only happened twice in all of her fifty-mumble years, and it hadn't been her fault either time. "I found a dog running around and I was wondering if you could get me in touch with his people so I can get him back home. He has a county license."

Penelope heard typing as Rochelle talked. "Oh, yeah, they're all out trying to catch loose dogs this morning, so all their calls are forwarding here. Pretty good windstorm last night, right? Between the trees falling down and whoever keeps lighting cars on fire, we were busy! Okay, what's the number on the tag?"

Penelope held her phone at a distance she could comfortably see and then read off the numbers.

There was more clattering from the keyboard, and then Rochelle spoke again. "Okay, I have a record. Little Yorkshire terrier named Purdue?"

"That's the one."

"Oh good. Sometimes these databases lie like you wouldn't believe. I have a phone number for the owner. Want me to transfer you through?"

Penelope thanked her. In the background, she could already hear another line ringing when Rochelle put her on hold to transfer the call.

The line Penelope had been transferred to clicked to an automated voice reciting a number. After the beep, she said her name and number and told them she had Perdue, and then managed to get her number in there again before it cut her off.

She looked at the dog in her arms, inciting another round of frenzied face licking. "Well, what are we going to do with you in the meantime?" She didn't have an extra leash with her, and Purdue looked like a dog that needed to be in a harness anyhow. There was only one thing she could do at the moment. She opened her mail bag and tucked the dog inside. "You have to promise you won't piddle on the mail, okay?"

Purdue panted and licked his nose. She supposed that was all the assurance she was likely to get.

Then Penelope dialed her husband's number as she headed toward the next house.

Jake picked up on the second ring. "You never call me when you're delivering mail. Is everything okay?" He drew in an audible breath. "Tell me you didn't find another body." Before Penelope could say anything, he laughed. "I'm kidding. What do you need?"

"It would serve you right if I *had* found another body." She dropped a handful of mail into the next mailbox, as far away as she could get from the big wolf spider. She slammed the top down. "But I didn't. However, I did find a dog, and I left a message with his people, but I don't know how long it's going to take for them to get back to me. Are you in the middle of something?"

"Just cleaning out the refrigerator. Do you have any idea what was in the square container with the orange lid? Is it supposed to be a liquid, or did it start in some other state?"

Penelope ducked under a branch that had fallen but not yet separated from the tree completely. "We don't have any orange lids. We have red lids and purple lids and even a pink lid, but nothing is orange. At least, it wasn't the last time I looked. You should probably treat it as hazardous waste." She scratched Purdue behind the ear as she flipped through the mail. "Don't feed it to Brutus."

"Yeah." Jake let that word drag out. "He's the reason I started this. Either the door didn't close completely or he's figured out how to get it open. Be prepared for some intestinal excitement this evening." He sighed. "You need me to come pick up the dog you found?"

"That would be great. He'll fit in the small crate in the spare bedroom." Penelope gave her cross streets.

"Do you think the owners of that dog would be interested in a swap?"

Penelope smiled as she opened the next mailbox and folded everything inside. "Don't let your dog get into the containers in the sink while you're gone."

Jake's answering laughter warmed something inside her. "I'll be there in a few minutes. I'm bringing our dog with me. But think about that swap thing. It could work."

CHAPTER 2

*E*sther's yard had already been cleaned up by the time Penelope finished her route, dropped off the mail truck, and walked back. The deadhead roses had been removed, all the paths raked, and new shredded redwood bark had been added atop the existing mulch. Even the porcupine sculpture that held tiny pots with succulents had been wiped down.

"It's looking good," Penelope said as she followed Esther back to the kitchen and sat at the table. "I thought you might need help picking up after the storm, but it looks like you're on top of things." Penelope hadn't noticed any wheelchair marks near the paths out front, so presumably someone else had done the actual cleanup. But having taught multiple generations of neighbors how to read during kindergarten, Esther didn't lack for people willing to drop everything to help out.

Esther raised one eyebrow as she poured lemonade from the pitcher. "Penelope, the last time you helped in my garden, I lost half my spinach starts and you dug up the daffodil bulbs."

Penelope remembered that day. "In my defense, you did ask me to weed that raised bed."

"Thin. Not weed. Thin." Esther shook her head. "Never mind. You have many other talents. Nobody is good at everything."

The calico jumped into Penelope's lap and sniffed at her shirt. "Yes, I was holding a dog," she told the cat. "Perdue the Yorkie," she added to Esther. "I found him huddling under a truck. I'm still waiting for his people to call back. He must have gotten out during the storm last night — along with half the other dogs in the neighborhood. Animal control seemed busy this morning."

Esther cocked her head. "Are you sure it was from the storm? At least three people at the rose garden meeting last night came home to find their dogs gone."

Penelope pushed her chin forward to let the cat rub against it while still maintaining eye contact with her friend. "You know as well as I do that half the fences in town fall over when we get strong winds. And the other half have gates that blow open unless they're latched perfectly."

Esther rolled her eyes. "Red and Sons strike again."

"Exactly." Red Anderson stayed in business by being the low bidder for any job, and he made a profit by hiring the completely unqualified. Two of his employees were his sons. Despite having worked in construction of some kind or another for twenty years, his sons routinely did work that left other professionals sighing and scratching their heads. But one of the other cost-saving measures of Red and Sons was not applying for permits, so no inspections were ever performed. Somehow, the city never quite caught up with them.

Faced with spending thousands to have a new fence put in, many homeowners elected to hire Red and Sons to "refurbish" the old fence. Obviously rotting posts would be replaced and termite-damaged slats swapped out. But the replacement wood might be weathered parts removed from another building site, and it was common for sections of the fence to sag to the ground the first time it rained. Red changed the company name every few years to stay ahead of angry clients.

"Plus, we had some thunder during the storm," Penelope added. "Even Brutus woke up for part of it." The mastiff had lifted his head once, rolled over, and gone back to sleep, but that was the most he ever reacted unless someone was coming near the house.

"Maybe." Esther frowned. "I'm starting to believe the rumor that the home garden show might be cursed this year. Everybody is having problems."

"Cursed beyond having hired Red and Sons to build their fences in the past?"

"Something dug up Aabira's lavender bushes — you know how nice those look lining the path. And now they're half-dead. And Pierre's father-in-law accidentally drove in reverse, went straight over the lawn, and killed the jacaranda."

Penelope nodded slowly and tried to figure out how to word her objection. "Pierre's father-in-law who is in his nineties? The one who had his license suspended last year? That father-in-law?" The license suspension had happened after the man in question had entered the freeway going the wrong direction. The entire town breathed a sigh of relief when his car had been sold.

"He found the keys to the family minivan and decided to go to the store to get more coffee. That in itself is a sign of the curse. Pierre hid those keys in a zipped pocket of his jacket that he kept in his own closet." When Penelope continued to look at her, Esther relented. "Okay, fine, maybe that one isn't a sign. But Aabira's lavender bushes may never recover. And what about all the cars burning?"

Penelope took a long drink of lemonade. "I'm pretty sure that's just vandalism. Or someone is retaliating for something." She didn't miss Jake's long hours when he'd still been on the police force, but she regretted no longer having all the extra information about what went on in town. "Do you know whose cars have been burned? Are they connected, or is it just a random thing?"

"No connection that I know of. One was a rental car. Two nights ago, it was a carpet cleaning van. The night before that, it was a brand new motorcycle. Last week it was a camper van." Esther stroked the orange tabby who had jumped into her lap. "It feels like there's a purpose in its randomness, if that makes any sense."

Penelope stood up, cat draped over one arm. "I don't see who profits from burning cars, but I'll run it by Jake to see if he has any thoughts." She set the cat down on the floor and headed back the hall.

Esther followed behind her in her wheelchair. "You don't suppose this is some sort of serial killer thing, do you? Isn't arson one of the signs? And animal cruelty. I hope that's not why all the dogs have gone missing."

Crouching over the first litter box, Penelope moved the scoop in a practiced motion, letting the clean sand fall back down. "Maybe Red and his sons are secretly serial killers and they build terrible fences that fall over so nobody finds out they take all the dogs." She finished one box and moved to the next as three cats jumped into the newly cleaned litter box. "It could be some bored kid, but breaking glass is more satisfying when you're a teenager. I'd be surprised if somebody isn't making money from the arson. Maybe it's related to some insurance scam."

"People often do try to make money from insurance

scams," Esther agreed. "Fine. I'll put my serial killer theory on the back burner for now. How is your yard coming along?"

Penelope laughed. "My yard? I was good enough to help dig up the grass, but once we got to the planting stage, it was Jake's yard again." After years of resistance, Jake had finally agreed to replace the lawn in front of the house with more drought-tolerant plants. "I think he's given each plant a name. He was out there yesterday measuring the slope and calculating water runoff. He's even started talking about French drains."

"We'll get him on the Rose Garden Committee eventually." Esther sounded satisfied.

Penelope shook her head. As long as Jake didn't hurt himself and eventually planted a pomegranate tree like he'd promised, she didn't particularly care what he did with the yard. The Rose Garden Committee might be a step too far, though. "I think he's done with dressing up to go to award ceremonies and fundraisers. You might have to set your sights on someone else."

"We'll see." Esther didn't sound particularly discouraged. "Bill Vaughn is talking about moving to a retirement community, so there may be an opening in a couple of years. Plenty of time to get your young man in shape for the challenge."

Penelope finished with the final litter box and started on a second round now the cats had all marked unclaimed territory. "I don't think Jake is ever going to be obsessive enough to win the slot for gardener of the year, so he would have to go after one of the elected positions. I have my doubts."

One spot in the committee was reserved for the winner of the best yard in the home garden show, and the other eight posts were elected for four-year terms. In some towns, finding nine people who wanted to be involved with the planning and maintenance of a rose garden next to the municipal library would be difficult enough, but the residents of Newtown had made the rose garden society into *the* prize that everyone wanted.

As the prestige had grown, so had the responsibilities, until the rose garden society was now in charge of park planning all over the city. The town's elected officials still needed to approve everything, but it was accepted that they would have to have a very good reason to go against the recommendations of the committee.

The last council member who had tried had been recalled halfway through his term.

"Never say never," Esther replied, and led the way back to the kitchen. As Penelope washed her hands, Esther opened her laptop. "I'm sending you pictures of the dogs that went missing during the meeting last night. Maybe you'll have better luck finding them."

"I'll keep an eye out. Hopefully, they just got scared by the storm and they've headed home." Penelope pushed her chair back under the table. "Do you need anything else? I have time to prune your rosebushes if you give me a pair of scissors." She grinned, waiting for Esther to look up in alarm.

Esther didn't even raise her head. "I'll see you tomorrow. Tell your young man to drop by if he needs any cuttings."

Penelope's smile widened as she headed for the door.

CHAPTER 3

Spending the early hours delivering mail meant dealing with the afternoon dog park people in order for Penelope to fulfill her pet sitting duties.

Mornings were usually perfect, with a mix of people who just wanted space to throw a ball for their dogs, and people who made the park one stop on their first walk of the day. Afternoons were a different thing entirely.

By the time Penelope arrived with Farlo and Lady, two miniature schnauzers who just wanted to chase a ball and each other, an entire raft of beach chairs had been set up in the little dog section and the afternoon crew was firmly settled in. Fifteen people were surrounded by a group of circling chihuahuas, poodles, and corgis. Penelope rather liked all the people as individuals, but when they got together and spent every afternoon discussing the failings of anyone not in earshot, they were intimidating. She suspected some people in the group only spent the entire afternoon because they were afraid of what might be said about them if they left early.

Over in the big dog section, divided from the small dog area only by a low chain-link fence, another five people sat at a picnic table, casting angry glances at the beach chair group. Penelope got Farlo and Lady through the double gate, unleashed them, and waved to the group in their beach chairs as she went by.

She thought she'd successfully run the gauntlet when she reached the far side, but after she threw the tennis ball for the schnauzers, a woman spoke from behind her.

"Did you hear about all the festival problems?" Linnea Kowalcik's flip-flops slapped against her heels as she hurried to catch up with Penelope. Her chihuahua, Britta, trotted along behind, collar jingling.

Farlo ran back with the ball, Lady two steps behind her, and Britta barked and snarled at them. The schnauzers ignored the tiny dog and waited for Penelope to throw the ball again. She obliged, then turned to face Linnea. "The missing dogs? I've seen the posters. You don't think it's just from the wind taking down fences last night?"

Linnea flipped her long hair to the side, the one bleached blond lock at her temple contrasting with the more natural dark brown underneath. As usual during nice weather, she wore shorts and a halter top, and she wore them with a confidence Penelope wished she had possessed when she was just turning thirty. The flip-flops and toe rings made her cringe a little — most people cleaned up after their dogs, but there was always someone who got to talking and didn't notice. Flip-flops just seemed like a bad idea in tall grass with possible piles of fresh dog poop. "No. If it was just fences going down, it would be a bunch of large dogs missing. Those people never bring their dogs inside when the weather gets bad."

Those people, in this context, didn't refer to a specific racial or ethnic group, but to large dog owners. Penelope wasn't sure if the divide had been exacerbated by the fence in the middle of the dog park or if the fence resulted from the divide, but she had heard the complaints on both sides. The small dog owners felt the big dog owners didn't take care of their animals adequately. The large dog owners thought the small dog owners forgot they had dogs and not children.

As someone who brought both large and small dogs to the park for her clients, Penelope tried to remain a neutral party. When it got too bad, she reminded herself about the years when they had been home to the "neutering is unnatural" brigade. *That* had led to multiple fights, people threatening to sue for public indecency, and one particularly cute unplanned litter of corgi and Great Dane puppies. The veterinary bills that came along with that birth had finally convinced multiple people to get their dogs fixed, or at least stop bringing them to the park.

Britta charged Lady and Farlo as they came back with the ball, and they continued to ignore her. "But why would *anyone* steal dogs?" Penelope tossed the ball again.

"Satanic rituals, obviously." When Penelope looked at her with one raised eyebrow, Linnea rolled her eyes. "I'm kidding. I just spent the weekend with my in-laws, and everything is either a sign from God or the devil tempting you. They weren't fans of my new tattoo." She pulled the halter top down to reveal what looked like vampire puncture marks and blood drops at the top of her left breast.

Penelope knew she should ask more about the missing dogs, but she couldn't help herself. "How did they even *see* that tattoo?" Anything other than a bikini top would have covered it.

Linnea grinned. "My mother-in-law insists on walking into the guest bedroom to open the curtains in the morning as soon as it's dawn, whether we're sleeping or not. I usually wear whatever full-length nightgown she's left out for me, but this time I just didn't feel like it." She let the fabric move back to its previous place. "I'm not sure what shocked her more — me sleeping in the nude or the tattoos. I do know that she's not going to be opening the curtains first thing in the morning the next time we stay over."

"Sounds like a win."

"Exactly." Linnea scowled at the group of people sitting at the picnic table on the other side of the park. "I don't know why those dogs are missing, but it's odd that they belong to a bunch of the rose garden volunteers." She glared at one man on the other side of the fence. "I'd say it was that ass Iain, but he was there being annoying until the end. God, I can't wait until we get the new rec center built and there's room for everyone to sit down during those meetings." She shrugged. "And it's not just the dogs. People's gardens are being dug up by animals, and nothing about the event seems to be going right. The flat butt brigade back there thinks the whole thing might be cursed." That last part was said with a laugh.

Penelope ignored the chihuahua snarling at the schnauzers again and picked up the ball. "Are you competing in the home garden show?"

"Not me. My husband, Tom. I just go to the meetings to make sure he doesn't drain our bank account to buy the newest hybrid rose that is almost black, or worse, sign us up to host something." She shook her head. "Last weekend was the first time he hasn't spent the entire time messing around in the yard, and we spent it at his parents' house." She looked over at the gate connecting the two sides of the park and raised her voice. "Hey! No dogs over thirty pounds on this side of the park!"

Penelope kept an eye on the gate while she threw the ball

again. Iain Hotz, his slightly too-long hair making him look like the community college English professor he was, had opened the gate to let his elderly golden retriever through. Barnaby had to be at least twice the weight limit for the little dog side, but Penelope was fairly certain even the smallest and most pampered of the chihuahuas in the area could take him in a fight.

Iain closed the gate behind him. "Barnaby isn't going to hurt anyone. And he's getting run over on the other side."

Linnea moved across the grass toward him, flip-flops clicking as she walked. "It doesn't matter. If people ignore the rules, it's the little dogs that are going to get hurt."

Penelope picked up the ball Lady had dropped at her feet and tossed it again. Britta had followed Linnea. Penelope winced, waiting for the chihuahua to go after the golden retriever, but Britta just sniffed Barnaby's face, licked his mouth once, and then sat next to him in the grass. Meanwhile, Linnea loudly recited the rules listed on the gate into the dog park, and Iain mimicked her gestures.

Three members of the beach chair flotilla got to their feet and started across the grass. When they saw that, everyone still seated at the picnic table stood up.

Penelope picked up the ball. "Sorry kids, we're going to have to cut things a little short today." Not that she suspected things would get violent, but people shouting at each other weren't watching their dogs, and even the best dogs needed to be monitored at the dog park.

She waved to the people still sitting down on her way out. Most of them were watching the drama happening thirty feet away with amusement, but two people were still scrolling on their phones.

Clipping leashes on the two schnauzers, Penelope gave them extra chest scratches. "We'll take the long way back to your house. They're mixing manure with compost at the big blue house. All the other dogs give it five stars. You'll love it."

Lady and Farlo trotted next to her as she went out the gate. Penelope glanced back before they rounded the corner and saw a mass of people, all speaking loudly and gesticulating. At the side of the action, Barnaby and Britta lay on the grass together, watching it all.

CHAPTER 4

The sun cast longer shadows when Penelope caught up to Jake at the rose garden parking lot, where he had been given the emergency task of setting up festival booths. He was staring at a plastic bag of bolts and nuts, wearing a t-shirt, shorts, leather gloves, and steel-toed boots — a combination Penelope found unaccountably attractive. "Hey, sexy. You free tonight?"

"Only if my wife doesn't find out." He looked up and did an exaggerated double-take. "Oh, it's you!" He leaned over and met her kiss halfway. "Glad you're here. You can help me figure this out. There aren't any instructions."

Three other men were staring at separate piles of lumber and hardware in the parking lot.

Penelope had the advantage of having seen the assembled booths many times. "The long four by fours go vertically on the front corners and hold the sign between them. After that, we might have to wing it." She looked around. "What happened to the crew that was supposed to do this?"

Jake laughed and pulled out the longest posts, positioning them about six feet from each other. "I'll let Esther tell you the whole story, but from what I heard, whoever was supposed to organize this area completely flaked on it, and nobody found out until this afternoon. We had to break into the shed where this was all being stored, and..." He gestured at the parking lot. "Esther called everyone who owns tools and wasn't already doing something else." He glanced up. "Before you feel excluded, I think she called me because I was the one most likely to be close to our toolbox and you were off walking dogs."

"It hadn't even occurred to me," Penelope lied. She sorted through the blue painted boards until she found both one by sixes that advertised the duck pond game and handed them over. "These go across the top."

Jake put them face down on the asphalt and sorted through the bag until he had picked out four of the longest bolts with washers and nuts attached. "That means these ones must be what we use here." He threaded them through and attached the nuts loosely. "How did your afternoon go?"

"I stayed out of the rumble at the dog park. It was like the sharks and jets, except stupider and with less dancing." Penelope pondered the other one by sixes, trying to remember exactly how the booth had looked. It was amazing how many times she had seen it without actually paying attention.

"The dancing is the only good part anyhow." Jake picked out his socket wrench and started tightening the bolts.

"I did get to see Linnea's new tattoo though." Penelope pulled out three of the planks and brought them over to him. "Not really my style, but I don't think I was the intended audience, anyway. Here, try these across the bottom. I think the whole thing is pretty low so the little kids can see over it."

After the first plank was secured, the second didn't fit. Jake unscrewed the first one and started trying them in a different order. "Whoever built these did *not* know what they were doing."

"Hush." Penelope went back to staring at planks. "If anyone hears you say that, you'll be in charge of building the next set." Around the parking lot there were sounds of wood being dropped on the ground, an electric drill, and swearing. "Pick up the pace a little. They're gaining on us."

"Using power tools is cheating." The ratcheting clicks of his socket wrench sped up. "What was the problem at the dog park?"

"The usual. Big dog in the little dog space." Now that half the lumber was in place, it was easier to see how the rest of it was supposed to go. She started laying everything out. "Any problems getting Purdue back to his people?" She had been in the middle of her daily jog with a German Shepherd when the lost dog's owner had called back. Jake had been tasked with taking the Yorkie home.

"Almost got licked to death. By the dog, not the owner. His owner gave me a bag of bulbs and she promised to bring cookies tomorrow."

Cookies were always a nice gesture, but the bag of bulbs made Penelope wonder. "Is it weird that at least three of the dogs that went missing last night are owned by people who were at the rose garden meeting?"

"That does seem a little unusual, yes." Jake dug more bolts out of the bag. "But that *was* when the winds kicked up. Maybe everyone else was home with their dogs indoors."

Across the parking lot, a sudden bout of swearing was followed by an electric drill running in reverse. Jake's quiet "Heh!' made Penelope grin. She watched the play of muscles under his t-shirt as he worked. "That's what *I* said, but half the people I've talked to today are convinced there's a conspiracy. Or a curse." She looked around at the piles of lumber. The only curse she could see here was poor planning.

"No offense, hon, but half the people you talk to on any given day are half a brick shy of a full load."

"So you're saying I attract those sorts of people?"

"I wasn't going to put it like that, but yes." Jake suddenly stopped and laughed. "I walked straight into that one, didn't I?" He went back to threading the bolt through the next set of boards.

"You'll find that other half brick someday."

"Pretty sure I already did." He crouched. "Can you lift that side? Too much pressure at the wrong spot and this thing is going to collapse into a stack of toothpicks."

Penelope helped him raise the wobbly front of the booth and then held it in place as he attached more boards. She looked at the gaps between the planks. "I've seen this construction before."

"So have I." Jake placed two planks side by side and eyed the place one of them was supposed to fit. "The neighbor in the back hired Red to replace the section he burned down, setting off fireworks. It was before you and I met," he added, tossing one of the boards to the other side of the structure. "The fence lasted almost three months before it fell over. I lured Brian over with a couple six-packs of beer and we spent a Saturday doing it properly."

Penelope looked at him in amazement. "You and Brian could make a killing if you ever decided to go into the fence building business. Brutus has slammed into that thing more than a few times and it's never even budged."

"I don't think my liver could handle that much beer every day, but I'll tell Brian you're impressed the next time I talk to him." Jake had helped his friend move out of state for his new job a few weeks ago, and they still talked on the phone nearly every evening.

A sky blue Mercedes Benz SUV drove over the cones blocking the parking lot entrance and threaded between the stacks of lumber before parking. Penelope had seen that SUV before, so she wasn't surprised to see Isolde Woodhouse emerge from the driver's seat. With the tight skin that only surgery could provide, Isolde prided herself at having been on the rose garden committee longer than anyone else. She looked like she could be sixty, but she'd looked sixty for at least the last twenty years.

While Isolde retrieved her shih tzu, Guinevere, from the special dog seat on the passenger side, Isolde's grandchildren emerged from the back. Both in their thirties, Tamsin and Leo were known around town for being Isolde's relatives and not much else. Together they had run a string of failed businesses — a restaurant, then a bookstore, then a yoga studio, and finally an art gallery — with investors who were only willing to join when Isolde cosigned the loans. Penelope had seen a sign on a vacant store downtown announcing a micro brewery a few months back, but construction seemed to have stalled.

Leo moved to one side of his grandmother and gestured to the arch Penelope was holding up. "See? I told you we had it under control, Gran."

The clicks of Jake's socket wrench slowed. "We?" He said it softly enough that only Penelope could hear it. Then he shook his head and went back to work.

Across the parking lot, a board clattered onto a pile with more force than necessary.

Isolde walked over to one of the piles nobody had started working on yet. The shih tzu's collar glittered every time Guinevere moved her head. "But this all should have been done already. By this time in the afternoon, they should already be hanging all the prizes."

Jake's hands stilled, and he looked up at Penelope. "Prizes? Esther didn't say anything about prizes. There's a little pool and a bag of plastic ducks for this booth, but that's it. I'm not even sure the pool will hold water."

Tamsin took Isolde's other elbow and tried to turn her back to the SUV. "I told you, Gran. There was a mixup with the shipping, but it's all going to get here tomorrow by ten."

Isolde stopped walking. "Ten? The booths open at eight."

Leo looked around the parking lot. "Well... if we want to have prizes here by eight, Tamsin and I will have to go buy them tonight. But that's not going to be in the budget."

Isolde's next words were lower in volume, as if she were gritting her teeth. "And how much will *that* be?"

"Fifteen hundred should be enough to see us through until the real order arrives. And of course, that will leave us with extra prizes at the end that we can use next year."

Isolde shrugged off Tamsin's hand and walked down the row of unmade booths in silence, heels of her stylish yet supportive shoes clicking on the asphalt. She didn't meet Penelope's gaze as she walked by. At the end of the row, she turned to face Leo and Tamsin, who had followed her one step behind. "Fine. But I want receipts." She headed back to the SUV at a faster pace. When Isolde went around the SUV to put the dog in her car seat, Leo and Tamsin high-fived each other and gave silent fist pumps of approval.

Jake got to his feet and stood next to Penelope. "I hope those kids have saved some of the money they've been stealing from her, because I don't think she's as oblivious as they think she is."

CHAPTER 5

*B*y eight thirty the next morning, Penelope had already spent half an hour cuddling with the reverend CJ Miller's elderly Dalmatian while the Episcopal priest conducted services, taken her own dog around the block to encourage whatever he had eaten in the refrigerator to make its way out, and was now at the home of her first real client of the day — CJ didn't count, since she charged him in pastries, not cash — to take Bella for a walk.

Bella's owner, Carol, spent her Fridays with her mother, who was allergic to dogs. Or at least, her mother was allergic to Bella. Since Bella was thirteen pounds of rage compressed into the body of a Pomeranian and had been banned by two groomers and a hardware store, Penelope had some doubts about the allergies.

Penelope dealt with Bella by letting her call the shots as long as nobody was getting hurt. Her theory was that if Bella wanted to go for a walk, she would eventually come over to have her harness put on. It usually worked. Some days Bella snarled at her for five minutes first, but Carol didn't mind if the walk was short as long as Bella made it outside at some point.

As expected, Carol's front garden was immaculate, with no hint of a stray weed or fallen branch to mar the beauty of the spiral of flowers that was the centerpiece. The police cruiser parked in front of the house was the only thing that didn't belong. Penelope discarded her first thought, that Bella had bitten someone. That would bring animal control, not the police. She considered staying outside and calling to see if Carol still needed her to walk Bella today. But if Carol needed to talk to the police about something, getting Bella out of the house might be the safest option for everyone. Penelope knocked on the door.

Her second surprise was the silence that greeted her knock. On a normal day, Bella would be growling and scratching at the panels until she recognized Penelope. This time there was nothing until Carol opened the door. Her eyes were red and puffy, and her long auburn hair had been pulled back into a messy ponytail, a departure from the usual sleek bun. "Oh. Penelope." She dabbed at her eyes with a tissue and seemed at a loss for what to do.

"Is everything okay? What happened?"

"Somebody took Bella!" At the last word, Carol started sobbing. She stepped back and Penelope followed her inside to where the town's most junior patrolman stood in the kitchen, fidgeting with a pen.

"Somebody *took* Bella?" Penelope repeated. "On *purpose?*" She winced as she heard her own words. "I mean, are you sure she just didn't get out somehow?"

The patrol officer stood up straighter and held his pen over his notebook, obviously realizing he was in danger of losing control of the conversation. "And you are…?"

"Penelope Standing."

"She's my dog walker," Carol added.

Penelope could see that her name meant something to him, but he was having a hard time coming up with the right context. She decided not to confuse the issue by making the connection for him. Though the notice had been hidden on the last page of the local paper, between a piano recital and the unveiling of the newest street sweeping machine, his swearing-in ceremony had taken place after Jake had retired. This officer's loyalty would be with the current head of the department, Chief Purcell. Since Purcell disliked Penelope, the conversation would probably go better if she just kept quiet about her husband being the former acting chief.

"And you have keys to the house?"

After digging in her pocket, Penelope pulled out the key, on its own labeled chain, the number 47 written on the paper encased in plastic. "I do." She turned to Carol. "When did she disappear?"

"This morning while I was helping with the final cleanup of the library garden before the festival. We had to sweep and rake before all the visitors showed up today." Carol gestured to the pink silk dog bed in the dining room. "She was in her bed when I left right before seven, and when I came back at eight, the front door was open and she was gone." Blotting her eyes again, she sniffed. "Normally I would have taken her with me, but there was supposed to be a big group doing the final walkthrough, and you know what Bella's like."

Penelope did indeed know what Bella was like.

The patrol officer tried again. "If you don't mind, I'd like to ask the questions here."

Still holding the key, Penelope raised her hands. "Of course. Sorry."

He looked at her over his notebook. "And where were you this morning between seven and eight?"

"Watching CJ's dog at the Episcopal church, and then I

went home and took my own dog for a walk. But the key was locked in the box with all the rest of them until ten minutes ago."

"Mm-hmm. And do you live alone?"

"No. I live with my husband."

He scribbled down more notes. "And was Mr. Standing with you this morning?"

Penelope wanted to laugh, but that felt insensitive with Carol right in the room, worried about her dog. "No. As far as I know, Jake doesn't have an alibi. That's Jake Wheeler." She spelled Jake's last name and watched the officer's eyes widen. "But we already have a dog, so I'm pretty sure he wouldn't have come over here to take Bella."

Brutus, the dog they had already, was bad enough, she wanted to say, but love was blind and Carol loved her Pomeranian. "I can give you Jake's number if you want to call and check." Penelope turned back to Carol. "But don't you have a key under the flowerpot?"

Penelope had never looked for a key in front of Carol's house. However, years of dealing with her clients had taught her that if there wasn't an alarm system, there would be a key under either a flowerpot or the doormat. Her own house was one of the few exceptions, and that was only because, after a long discussion, she had finally agreed with Jake that leaving the house key in such an obvious place set a terrible example for the assistant chief of police.

The hand not holding the tissue flew up to cover Carol's mouth. "Oh, that's right. I forgot all about that."

The officer's pen tilted away from the page. "There's a key outside?" He sounded incredulous. "Where anyone could get to it?"

Carol's eyes darted to the door. "I think so. I haven't looked in a while." She hurried away.

Penelope, left alone with the officer who looked like he

wanted to be just about anywhere else, shrugged. "It's pretty common around here. If it's not there, it's under the mat. Or in one of those fake rocks, but everyone got the fake rocks from the same place and for a while the kids thought it was funny to swap them with the same model from another house when they were on their way to school." After a few months, most of the victims had given up trying to find their own house key and had another one cut at the hardware store.

Carol came back, holding up the key. "Still there."

The officer flipped his notebook closed. "Ma'am, is it possible you didn't close the front door all the way when you left?"

Carol frowned at him. "Of course not. I always lock the door very carefully."

"But there's nothing else missing? Cash, jewelry, computers, that sort of thing?" He edged closer to the door. When Carol shook her head, he adjusted his duty belt. "Maybe the door blew open on its own. I'll make a note of this in case something comes up, but you should go to the shelter and see if anyone brought the dog in."

Penelope waited in the kitchen while Carol saw the police officer out and closed the door behind him. "I locked the door when I left. I know I did," she said as she came back into the kitchen.

"I believe you." Penelope really did believe her. She'd been walking Bella at least once per week for six months, and not once had the door been unlocked when she'd arrived. "Maybe someone broke in and Bella chased them off before they could steal anything. If they left the door open, she might have chased them down the street and then decided to take her own walk instead of coming right home."

"But she could be out there, hit by a car!"

"She has her collar on with your phone number, right? If she were injured, somebody would have called by now." If Bella was uninjured, nobody would be able to get close enough to read the phone number without taking their life into their own hands. "Go ahead and call the shelter now. Let them know she's missing and see if anyone has reported a loose dog matching her description. I'll take a quick tour of the neighborhood and see if I can find her, okay?"

* * *

THIRTY MINUTES LATER, PENELOPE WAS BACK AT CAROL'S house, helping her client create a lost dog poster. Bella hadn't been at any of the places she liked to go on walks, and Penelope had looked carefully in the streets and curbs, finding nothing other than leaves and branches leftover from the storm.

"I think someone stole her," Carol said for the fifth time. "Why else would there be no sign of her? I don't think she would leave on her own."

Penelope stared at the screen, ostensibly reading over the poster while trying to figure out the least offensive way to word her objection. What she wanted to say was *Nobody else would want Bella* or *Who else would put up with that dog?* But that wasn't what Carol needed to hear. "Has anyone seemed particularly interested in her lately?"

"No." She looked even more depressed. "Maybe my mother hired someone to get rid of her. She doesn't like Bella."

Penelope strangled the laugh in her throat. "Carol, I've met your mother. I'm pretty sure she didn't take out a hit on your dog." She stood up. "I have to go, but I'll keep an eye out for her. Call me if you find her, okay?"

29

"Thank you."

On her way out of the area to go to her next client, Penelope took the long way around and spent a few moments checking the school playground for a small orange bundle of fur. But if Bella was hiding, she was doing a good job of it.

CHAPTER 6

*P*enelope knelt by the side door of the garage and re-inserted the tension wrench. "You can do this." With her other hand, she inserted the hook pick and tried to imagine the pins as she tapped them.

Picking a lock seemed so easy when she saw someone else do it. She'd spent many hours watching videos and practicing, and she was realizing why so many people just smashed windows and opened the door from the inside. The hook pick caught on something and she lost her grip on it. It tumbled down to the ground.

Again.

Penelope ignored the rumbling of her stomach. The next time was going to be the time that worked. It had to be. She had too many things to do to spend too much longer on this. She reset the tension wrench and started feeling around with the hook pick.

Jake's shadow cut the glare on the glass above the knob. "Do you want me to bring your lunch out here, or are you coming inside?"

"I've almost got it." The hook pick fell to the ground again. "This is going to be the time it all comes together."

"I believe in you." He paused. "But I left your lunch in the microwave, and Brutus is getting better at opening things, so I should probably go back inside."

Penelope closed her eyes and laughed. "I swear, every time I think he can't possibly get any worse, he clears the next bar." She picked up both tools and stood up. "Maybe tomorrow will be the day."

Trailing behind Jake on the way into the house, she turned back to the question she'd been thinking about as she worked on the lock. "Why would someone take a Pomeranian?"

Jake cleared his throat loudly. There was a thud as dog feet hit the tiled floor of the kitchen. "Because a mastiff is too hard to carry? Was that supposed to be a logic puzzle?"

"It wasn't supposed to be, but I like the way you think." They entered the kitchen to find a very innocent-looking Brutus stretched out on his bed in the corner. "Oh, look at the good dog who would *never* think about getting on the counter."

Jake looked in the sink. "I'm just going to call that the pre-wash cycle." He shook his head and opened the microwave. "I hope you're okay with the leftover chicken Kiev. It was either that or the seven levels of hell casserole." He put a plate down on the table for her.

"Thank you. Pretty sure it was called the seven layer vegetable casserole, but I agree, not a recipe I'm going to try again." She eyed him. "In fact, I'm a little surprised it hasn't accidentally fallen on the floor."

Jake never admitted to using Brutus to get rid of leftovers he didn't want to eat, but a suspicious percentage of failed new recipes made it into the dog's stomach before they could make it onto the table for another meal.

"I'm not sure I would survive the flatulence." He put another plate in the microwave and turned it on. "Are you going to tell me why you were asking about the Pomeranian, or was it just a random thought?"

During the minute and a half while Jake's food heated, Penelope told him about Carol, Bella, and the patrol officer who hadn't seemed interested in finding out what might have happened. She wrapped up her summary when he got up to retrieve his food. "Linnea said something yesterday at the dog park about how it was weird that a bunch of small dogs had gone missing. At the time I thought it was just another example of everyone wanting to jump on the 'the garden show is cursed' train, but now I'm starting to wonder."

"Because small dogs don't run away?" He sat down at the table across from her.

"Oh, no, they absolutely do. But they usually don't go quite so far. And Linnea is right — there aren't very many small dogs that are outside at night."

Jake turned to look at Brutus. "Are you telling me we could kick him outside when we go to bed and I could stretch my legs out?"

"No. Brutus is a lapdog in a large body. And you would feel so guilty if he was outside that you would sleep out there with him. But some people do have outside dogs, and those are usually the ones that get lost when fences fall over if the wind kicks up." Penelope put her fork down, pulled out her phone, and brought up the pet sitting schedule. "Are you still taking Heidi for her run this afternoon, or has Esther conned you into doing something for the festival again today?"

"Both. Heidi and I are going for a run at two. I'll be back in time for the mulch to be delivered at three thirty, and then I get to run the fish pond booth from five to eight." He leaned forward to squint at her phone. "If you need me to take some of those, I can."

"Excellent initiative by the intern," Penelope noted, "but I've got it. You didn't put the mulch delivery on the calendar."

"No, I didn't put the mulch delivery on *your* calendar. Not after the paver delivery." He concentrated on his food for a few seconds before looking up with a grin.

Penelope pointed her fork at him. "The guy from the hardware store was being an ass just because I was a woman, and you know it." Their plans to redo the path along the side of the house had hit a snag when Penelope had picked out pavers and paid to have them delivered. The truck had shown up with the wrong kind, and the driver had insisted that Penelope call her husband to check on the order.

Things had gone downhill from that point, though Jake had been the one to tell the driver to leave in the end. They still hadn't redone the path along the side of the house. Penelope thought it might have turned out for the best; now that the front was being redone, it would be nice to tie the two parts together with a different type of stone.

Jake nodded. "This is my 'I'm not disagreeing with you' face, but we really need the mulch today or Esther is going to be disappointed in our yard. You don't want Esther to be disappointed, do you?"

Penelope glared at him. "Fine. But only because I want Esther to be happy." She stood up. "Do you want a cookie?"

Brutus jumped to his feet and ran to her.

"Not you. But that was my fault for saying one of the magic words." Brutus's vocabulary was almost entirely food related and growing daily. Penelope pulled a treat from her pocket and gave it to him. "Go lie down and behave yourself." She pulled down the cookie tin from over the refrigerator. "Jake?"

"Yes, please."

Penelope removed two cookies from the tin and went back to the table. "The duck pond booth, hm?"

"For some reason, nobody wanted to work that one, so I told Esther I'd be happy to. What am I missing?"

"Bring something low to sit on so you don't have to spend the whole time crouched over. And try not to scare the children."

"I would never." He set his cookie on the edge of his plate while he finished the chicken. "So do *you* think there's something to the garden show curse, or just some bad luck?"

"Definitely not a curse, but I'm not convinced this is just a string of bad luck. It's weird that so many of the dogs are owned by rose garden society members. I just can't figure out why someone would steal dogs." She picked the burned chocolate chip off the edge of the cookie and ate it. "I don't think Purcell is going to spend much effort looking into it."

"To be fair, the burned cars probably *should* be a higher priority than dogs that might have gotten out on their own," Jake said. His face stayed carefully neutral. He didn't like the new police chief any more than she did, but he was a lot more careful about showing it. "The zone five serious crime stats are going to crater." Then he grinned. "I'm glad I'm not the one who has to present that report to the city council next month."

"Ah, I knew the schadenfreude had to show up at some point. Still okay with your decision to leave?"

"I'm still enjoying being the pet sitting intern, if that's what you're asking." He looked at the schedule. "Though we're not *quite* busy enough to need two people. Who knows, maybe I'll have so much fun attaching plastic fish to fishing poles I'll decide the carnie life is my future."

"You have clearly never worked at a small carnival. The stories I could tell about the PTA carnivals would curdle your blood."

Jake smiled and kept eating.

"You think I'm kidding." Penelope shook her head. "Just you wait."

Jake stood up, cookie in hand, and took both plates to the sink. "Can I use the garage door now, or are you going to swear at it some more?"

"It's all yours. I have to get going — assuming all of my clients haven't had their dogs stolen. Enjoy your mulch."

"You know I will."

Penelope paused to throw Brutus a treat and kiss Jake on the cheek and then slipped out the door.

CHAPTER 7

*P*enelope knocked on Esther's door, half expecting her to be out looking at the gardens in the neighborhood, but her friend opened the door, a cordless phone held between her neck and ear, and gestured Penelope inside. "No, I'm still here, Jillian. Do you know where Bill went?" She paused. "Well, you would know better than I would."

Esther's call sounded important enough that Penelope didn't want to disturb her, so she slipped by the wheelchair and headed back the hall. Three of the cats hurried into the back room with her. She obliged them by throwing the ball for Duke and waving the feather wand around for Spider and Malted Milk for a few minutes. After she had scooped the litter boxes and swept the stray sand off the floor, Penelope headed back to the kitchen to wash her hands.

Esther was just putting the phone back in its cradle. "Honestly, I don't see how some people make it to their seventies without learning anything at all. Jillian and Bill's dog, Briar, went missing during the windstorm. Someone called them saying he has Briar, but he needs money or he's never going to bring her back. And of course Bill just charges off to go buy gift cards and won't answer his phone." She shook her head. "The senior center just had a presentation about gift card scams last month."

Penelope turned off the water and dried her hands. "Did it sound like he really had their dog?"

"Jillian said he knew Briar's name and knew she was a dachshund, but..."

Penelope sighed. "That's on the posters I've been seeing all morning. Do you know where Bill was going to buy gift cards? Maybe I can get there and talk him out of it."

Esther shook her head. "Not necessary. Jillian just put a 24 hour hold on their credit cards and ATM card. Bill never has more than fifteen dollars in cash, so this crisis has been averted. At least until they get some proof that this guy has Briar and she's okay." She sighed. "Of course, if this person *has* Briar, I'm sure they'll drain all their accounts to get her back."

Penelope sat down at the kitchen table and accepted a glass of lemonade. "I know the police probably aren't going to do anything, but it might be worth telling them anyway. And we need to let everyone else whose dogs are missing know that someone is running this scam." She pulled out her phone. "I'll let Carol..." She paused, trying to remember Carol's last name. She could remember all the dog's health issues and allergies, but the owner's surname escaped her. "Bella's mom. She has the flowers in a spiral?"

"Entweiler."

"Yes, thank you." Penelope composed a message and sent it off.

In the meantime, Esther had opened her tattered address book and flipped through the pages before dialing. "Isolde? It's Esther. No, I'm sorry, I don't have any news."

Penelope drank her lemonade as she waited for Esther to explain the scam. After Esther had put the phone down,

Penelope spoke. "When did Guinevere disappear? I just saw Isolde last night when Jake was putting the booths together."

"Early this morning. As if Isolde needs another thing to worry about. She wanted to have her grandchildren take over some responsibilities this year so she could transition to more of a ceremonial role, but they've just caused twice as much work and stress. Isolde has been planning on taking a cruise from Norway to Greece and then back again, but I think she's realizing that if she does that, the rose garden committee is going to need to get someone else first." Esther shook her head and started paging through her address book. "Anyhow, Isolde is trying to keep focussed on the festival."

"Have you heard of anyone whose dog is missing who *isn't* part of the rose garden society?"

Esther paused, phone in hand. "Well, no. But almost everyone I know is part of the rose garden society in some capacity. Even you, and you have the blackest thumb I've ever seen." She smiled at Penelope. "You try, I know." She stared at the address book for a moment, then looked up again. "I know of one *cat* that went missing that's owned by someone not part of the club, but that's it. What do dogs and the rose garden society have to do with each other?"

"Nothing that I can think of." Penelope stood up. "But I think it's very interesting, don't you? Something odd is going on."

CHAPTER 8

The dump truck with six cubic yards of shredded redwood mulch had just backed into the driveway when Penelope turned the corner onto her own street. She could smell the earthy undertones of the wood two houses away. Jake waited in the front yard with a leashed Brutus.

Penelope scratched the dog's chest and kissed her husband. "I thought I might not get here in time to be patronized, but Biggie decided he was hungry today, so I didn't have to spend twenty minutes trying to get him to eat before I gave his insulin."

"I'm glad you're here. I have a surprise for you."

Standing further up the driveway, a man in his thirties wearing a t-shirt with the stylized RT Landscaping logo matching the one on the dump truck whistled sharply. "That's good," he yelled to the driver. Then he moved to the side as the front of the truck bed rose.

Shredded bark tumbled onto the driveway, clumping together to form large shapes that were submerged as the rest fell on top of them. Penelope raised her voice to be audible over the whine of the hydraulic lift. "This is exciting and all, but I was there when you ordered it."

"That's not the surprise. Give it a few minutes."

Penelope watched as the mountain of mulch kept growing. "That seems like… a lot." Spreading it out everywhere was going to take a while. "Are you sure you calculated the amount correctly?"

The bed of the truck stayed raised to its highest point and the man outside used a rake to get the last bit off the back and onto the mound covering most of the driveway. He signaled again and the truck bed lowered.

Jake raised an eyebrow and looked at Penelope. "It's a simple math equation. The area that needs to be covered times the depth you want, and then converted into cubic yards."

"Yes, but…" Penelope looked at the mountain of mulch. "It just seems like a lot," she repeated.

"It will go down quickly." He waited expectantly as the dump truck bed went back to its normal position. When the engine cut out, the quiet was noticeable. The driver's door opened and someone came walking around the front. "This is the surprise."

Expecting an older version of the man with the rake, instead, Penelope saw a woman striding toward them. Dressed in jeans and heavy boots, she walked with authority. She held up the clipboard. "Who wants to sign?"

Penelope pointed to Jake. "His name is on the order." She lowered her voice. "Next time I get to order the mulch."

Jake smiled and handed Brutus's leash to her. He took the clipboard and started reading the agreement, and Penelope gave Brutus a treat because he hadn't jumped on the driver yet.

The driver focussed on Brutus. "He looks like a handful. Can I say hello?"

"As long as you don't mind a little drool." Penelope grinned as the other woman laughed loudly and gestured to her work clothes. "This is Brutus."

Brutus took that as his invitation to launch himself forward, which sent them both to the ground, but the woman was scratching the dog's belly so Penelope assumed she was okay with it. Now that she got a better look at her, Penelope realized her first assumption had been partially correct — she *was* an older version of the man with a rake, but with a ponytail instead of a beard. Halfway buried under the mastiff, the driver looked up at the person who had to be her son. "Now *this* is a dog, Rufus." Her son briefly paused in strapping the rake back in place, the only sign he had heard her, then got into the passenger seat. The driver turned her face so Brutus was licking her cheek instead of her mouth and reached her hand up to Penelope. "Rebecca Tinsdale."

Penelope shook her hand. "Penelope Standing. You're a fan of large dogs?"

"The larger the better. Nobody's going to disappear with a dog like this." She extricated herself from under Brutus, stood up, and gestured at the mulch pile. "You folks left it a little late for the garden show, didn't you? I thought we were done for the season two days ago."

Penelope nodded. "Last year this was all grass, and we didn't realize how scandalous an unmulched garden would be." It was only when Esther had asked her when they had scheduled the delivery that Penelope had realized the error of their ways. "I hadn't quite pictured the amount we would be getting."

Rebecca laughed. "It'll go quickly, though it might not feel like it after the first few hours." She took the clipboard back from Jake, detached the bottom copy, and handed it to him. "Enjoy your weekend." She crouched down to pet Brutus's belly. "You be a good boy."

Penelope leaned into Jake and watched Rebecca start the truck and drive off. "Do you think she might need someone to take over the deliveries when she's on vacation?"

"You'd have to get your class B commercial license first." Jake slipped an arm around her. "I thought you might enjoy that."

The dump truck slowed to take a corner, then was gone from view. Penelope sighed. "After I take all your money and leave you a shallow husk of a man, I think I want to learn how to drive construction equipment."

Jake patted her stomach. "Solid plan. Let me know what I can do to help."

"Deal." Penelope looked at the driveway. "But first, we should probably do something about that. How much do you think we can get done in an hour?"

"Let's find out."

With both of them working, they got a third of the mulch distributed around the front garden. It wasn't at the three-inch depth Jake had calculated, but at least it contrasted nicely with the plants and gave the whole area a pleasing appearance. Though they weren't in any danger of winning an award, Penelope thought Esther wouldn't disown her either.

Then Penelope had to run off to take care of some pets. By the time she caught up with Jake at the carnival, she'd fed and scooped boxes for two more cats, given fluids to a dog, walked Brutus on the short version of their two most common routes, and then taken a well-deserved and much-needed shower.

The rose garden carnival area reminded her of the grade school PTA functions she'd been a part of — a relief for the parents who wanted to talk to adults, somewhat entertaining for the little kids, and more than a little embarrassing for the older children. The teens clustered together, typing on their phones.

Penelope purchased a pack of twenty-five tickets from

the booth, assuming she wouldn't use more than ten of them. It was all for a good cause. Besides, Loren Hardy was watching from a seat nearby, and Penelope didn't want rumors of an impending bankruptcy to start because she hadn't bought enough tickets.

At the duck pond booth, Jake sat on a step stool, reading a book and eating popcorn. A flotilla of battered plastic ducks with metal disks epoxied to their backs bobbed in the wading pool behind him. On another step stool, a cardboard box of cheap, individually wrapped toys showed a high tide mark where it had absorbed water earlier in the day.

Penelope put one ticket down on the ledge and picked up the fishing pole, a two foot wooden dowel with a string stapled onto it. A magnet dangled from the other end of the line. "How's it going?"

Jake put his book down, ripped her ticket in half, and dropped it into a box by his feet. "Most of the little kids already came by earlier in the day, so it's been quiet." He watched as Penelope dangled the magnet over a waterlogged duck missing most of its paint. "But there was a line for a little while after one mother came back and complained the cowboy toy was obscene. Then we ran out of the cowboys, so I had to retire duck five and everyone left again."

Penelope raised an eyebrow.

He shrugged. "I'd say poor manufacturing and an unfortunate color choice, but you don't have to have too much imagination to see it. I saved one for you."

"Language of love, right there." She managed to attach the magnet to her chosen duck, but the attraction wasn't strong enough to lift the plastic animal with the weight of the water inside. "Can you rescue my drowning duck, please?"

Jake leaned over and picked it up, holding it over the pool to let it drain before showing her the number on the bottom. "Lucky number twelve! Nobody's picked that one yet." He dug through the cardboard box and picked out a bag with the number written on it. He started to hand it to her, then stopped and looked more closely. Closing his eyes, he laughed.

Penelope smiled, trying to hold the moment. Five years ago, she'd assumed she would be single for the rest of her life. She'd been content with that — she had friends and a community — but then Jake had come along, an unexpected gift she still sometimes couldn't believe.

Still laughing, Jake opened his eyes and handed her the bag. Inside was a plastic charm suitable for using as a key chain. The subject was two smiling pigs in top hats and canes, standing on their hind legs. The way the form had been made, the pigs were turned to the side, one slightly behind the other with no space between them. That wouldn't have been excessively suggestive, but the paint dabbed on for the eyes and mouth made it look like the pig in front was cross-eyed, possibly in the throes of passion.

Penelope looked at the bag in her hand. "I think maybe it's good that duck twelve has been so hard to pick up." She started giggling halfway through the sentence and almost couldn't finish.

"I think I'll just retire duck twelve right now." Jake rubbed his face. "I don't think I can handle another conversation like the last one."

Penelope tore off three tickets from her bundle and handed him the rest. "It would be a service to the community if you removed those from the box to protect the innocent children. I'm going to give them out as Christmas ornaments next year."

Jake put the box on his lap and started digging through it. "I should probably look at the rest of them while I'm at it. I'm surprised there weren't other complaints." He held up a turtle, squinted at it, then tossed it back in the box. After shaking out the last few bits of popcorn in his bag, he tossed two pig charms inside.

"What are the odds that two of them would have problems?" Shoving her new key chain charm into her pocket, Penelope stopped to reconsider her words. "Actually, what *are* the odds of that happening? It seems unlikely, but I can't imagine this would be on purpose."

Jake continued sorting through the box, plastic bags crinkling. "My guess is that someone at the toy company noticed, and Isolde's grandkids... What are their names again?"

"Tamsin and Leo."

"Ah, yes. I'd bet twenty bucks that Tamsin and Leo got a *great* deal on these prizes. Probably not on the receipt they gave to Isolde though." The popcorn bag sagged from the weight.

Penelope watched as more got added to the mature toys bag. "Someone's going to notice if you remove half the ducks."

"Not a problem. If it's for a kid, I'll just read out a different number. Nobody will notice." He nudged duck twelve with his foot. "I'm still going to leave this one out, though. It doesn't float."

"Sneaky. I like it." Penelope looked around. "I'm going to see what else is here and get something to eat. Do you want anything?"

Jake looked at the toy in his hand and started laughing again. He added it to the popcorn bag and then looked up. "Maybe some nachos? Without jalapeños."

Penelope nodded. "Back in a bit."

As she wandered away, two men came up to the booth with a little girl who couldn't have been older than five. Jake's voice carried across the space. "Lucky number... seventeen!"

The ring toss had off-brand stuffed animals that might get someone sued for trademark violations, but weren't likely to cause outrage. On the other side of that, Esther was collecting tickets at the water gun booth and there wasn't a line. Penelope handed over a ticket. "How are things going over here?"

"Don't pump it more than five times or the back of the gun falls off." Esther handed her a lime green water gun and reset the targets. "The turnout isn't too bad today. I think everyone showed up to see what happens in the cake walk this year." The previous year had ended with shoving and muttered swearing as people tried to avoid Janice Yarborough's cherry surprise cake. "Did Jake save you a cowboy?"

"He did. Have you seen the pigs yet?" Penelope dug the key chain out of her pocket and handed it to Esther. She pumped up the water gun and aimed. Her first blast missed all the targets.

In the distance she heard "Lucky number thirty-seven!"

Esther pulled her glasses on and looked at the pigs. "Ha! Oh, dear. The planning committee's never going to hear the end of it if too many children go home with these."

"If anyone complains, tell them they must have a dirty mind." The second blast hit a target but didn't knock it over. "Jake's over there separating the toys into young and mature prizes." She pumped the water gun again and aimed. The last of the water hit the target, and this time, it fell over. "Finally!"

Esther exchanged the water gun for a tiny unicorn stuffed animal that was missing half its fur.

Holding it up between two fingers, Penelope made a face. "At my house, this would be a foreign body waiting to happen. Do you want to take it home to your cats?"

Esther took the unicorn and tossed it back in the bin it had come from. "They're filled with those little foam beads that scatter everywhere. My cats would dismember it in less than five minutes and I would be vacuuming up foam beads for the rest of my life." She returned Penelope's key chain. "But I guess it could be worse."

"Silver linings everywhere." Penelope leaned closer. "Do you know if any of the dogs have turned up yet?"

"Not as far as I know. Isolde wanted to file a police report, but they referred her to animal services. She's trying to hire a private detective."

"Do they even do that sort of thing?"

Esther shook her head. "Apparently not. She's already called all the ones in the telephone book, and the minute they hear it's about a missing dog, they hang up." Her face took on a thoughtful look as she slipped off her glasses and stared at the duck pond booth where a line of teenagers had formed. "You know who has both time *and* detective experience?"

Penelope tried to keep a straight face. "If I were a good wife, I probably wouldn't laugh."

"If you didn't laugh about this sort of thing, he never would have married you." Esther pulled out the cell phone she only bothered turning on when she left her house. "Don't worry. I won't ask you to persuade him. I'll have Isolde talk to him." She pulled her glasses up again and started dialing.

Penelope glanced at the line in front of Jake's booth. Isolde couldn't possibly talk to him until the line went down. Penelope had time to get something to eat. Jake would handle a request like that better on a full stomach anyhow.

Leo and Tamsin hadn't been in charge of the food, so it was exactly what Penelope had expected. She was almost done eating the corn dog by the time she got to the front of the cotton candy line, and the orange cheese on the top of Jake's nachos had congealed. To protect him from such an unappetizing sight, Penelope ate the top layer of chips while she navigated the area behind the booths.

Jake looked up from taking tickets when she stepped past the wading pool and set the paper boat of chips and cheese next to him. "Thanks." He turned back to the teen in front of him. "Pigs, turtle, or rooster?"

The teen handed over a handful of tickets. "Three roosters and a turtle."

Jake dug through the popcorn bag and passed the desired items over. "Next! Pigs, turtle, or rooster?"

Penelope waited until there was a break in the line. "You seem to have cut out the ducks and just gone straight to the chase."

"Did you see that line? I didn't have time to screw around with the ducks." He looked at the nachos. "Order's a little light, isn't it? They're making a killing for what they're charging."

Penelope shrugged. "Maybe they're trying to keep everyone healthy. Cholesterol is the silent killer, you know."

Jake paused with a chip halfway to his mouth. "Pretty sure that's high blood pressure."

"They aren't connected?"

"Who knows?" He ate the chip and swiped his thumb across her chin. "Little bit of cheese there, hon."

Penelope grinned, leaned forward, and kissed him. "Just looking out for you." She sat back. "Speaking of which…"

"Hold that thought." He held up one finger and turned his head. "Pigs, turtle, or rooster?"

"One of each."

A crinkle of plastic accompanied the exchange. "Tell your friends we're almost out, so now is the time if anyone wants more."

Penelope waited until the customer had moved away. "Are you really almost out?"

"Getting close. And if I get rid of all of these, I'm shutting the booth down early. None of the little kids are going to be here late." He looked into the popcorn bag. "I hate to say it, but these things may have been a stroke of genius. I was told I'd pull in about twenty tickets on a good night, and I've more than quadrupled that already." He looked up at the young woman on the other side of the booth divider. "Pigs, turtle, or... Nope, never mind. The roosters are all gone. Pigs or turtle?"

"Four turtles. I'm going to make my own stop-action show."

Jake froze, then shook his head. "Not even going to ask." He pushed the toys across the counter. "Good luck with the filming."

"Thanks."

Jake watched the auteur walk away before he turned back to Penelope. "You were about to say something."

"I just wanted to warn you..." She paused. "I'm waiting for you to get into your 'I can handle anything' pose."

He put another chip in his mouth and clasped his hands together on his knees. "Go ahead."

"It's about the missing dogs."

"Someone thinks *I* took them?"

Penelope brightened. "Nope. Great news! You are *not* a suspect."

Jake was starting to look a little suspicious. "So...?"

"Esther told me that Isolde tried to get the police to look into it."

Jake shook his head and held up his hands in a warding motion. "Oh, no. I'm not getting in the middle of that. I'm retired and they have a chief."

"Nope, not that either." She waited expectantly until he clasped his hands on his knees again. "Isolde wants to hire someone to find the dogs."

Jake stared at her. "What?"

An errant ring from the booth next door flew into the pool, knocking the ducks around. Penelope fished out the ring and handed it back to the person in charge. "It makes some sense when you think about it."

"Yes, but that's why there are private detectives." He turned to the balding man waiting in front of the booth and exchanged two turtles for tickets.

"Apparently they're too busy following cheating spouses."

Jake ate another chip. "You know the most likely thing is that animal control is going to find those dogs all running around in one of the unincorporated areas, right? And if they *didn't* all just get out on their own, the likelihood that I would be able to find them is almost zero."

"I'm sure Isolde knows that. But she has to do *something*." Penelope tore off a chunk of cotton candy and stuffed it into her mouth, enjoying the sensation of something dissolving into nothing. "What if Brutus disappeared?"

Jake raised one eyebrow. "Hon, if Brutus disappeared I'd use all the money we saved on our grocery bills and treat us to a really nice vacation."

"Awfully tough talk for someone who bought refrigerated sirloin dog treats." Having watched Jake carry the mastiff to the car and rush him to the veterinarian when the dog had torn off part of his nail, Penelope was confident his reaction if Brutus disappeared would be swift and unforgettable.

"High value training treats. He's going to earn it all back the first time he tracks a child who has fallen into a well." He sold another turtle. "What do you think about it?"

"Me? I think you're the best option, but only if it's something you want to do. I can go back to taking care of all the pet sitting clients for a while." Having two people made scheduling easier, especially on days when she delivered mail. But she'd done it all solo before he'd retired, and she hadn't added too many clients since then.

A little frown line appeared on his brow, a sure sign that he was thinking about the specifics. "I'm not a licensed P.I., so

I wouldn't be able to charge for it, but there's no reason I couldn't look into what happened to the missing dogs. At the very least we could talk to the owners and look for patterns."

"We?"

He shot her a look of disbelief. "You didn't honestly expect me to believe I'd be doing this on my own, did you?" He used a chip to scrape up the cheese at the bottom of the tub. "Besides, if this ever comes down to catching a bunch of little dogs in a field somewhere, I'm leaving it all to you."

Penelope smiled and tore off another chunk of the cotton candy. She looked out onto the path between the booths. "It sounds like you're interested. So I guess I don't need to warn you that Isolde is on her way over right now." She grabbed the bag with the last of the questionable toys. "I'll take over the booth for a while. You go work things out with Isolde."

CHAPTER 10

By early morning, everyone had heard Jake was investigating the disappearance of the dogs.

Even CJ, who was notorious for going to bed early so he would be well rested for the morning service, knew about it. He greeted Penelope and Jake as they came into the rectory kitchen, absently moving around the arthritic Dalmatian. "Coffee's still warm. I'll try to keep things moving this morning so you can go do your detecting."

Penelope sat down on the floor and let Spot sprawl on her legs while her husband poured the coffee. "Don't rush. If Jake shows up at anyone's door to talk to them before eight, they're probably going to call the cops on him." She accepted a mug from Jake. "I don't suppose you've heard anything about what happened to the dogs."

"Not a peep." He paused. "Or bark, as the case may be. It's such an odd thing, isn't it?" He gazed fondly at Spot. "They are worth so much to us, but in fact, they don't really have a resale value."

"Unless the scammers asking for payment really do have

the dogs." Penelope tugged on Spot's ear and the dog's tail slapped against the linoleum.

"Oh, yes, I heard about that. Esther wants to schedule another session on how to avoid scams." He sighed. "I'm afraid the people who come for those meetings aren't the ones who need them. Still, I suppose we have to try. And it gets people out of the house, which helps." He looked over at Jake, who was cleaning the empty coffeepot. "Help yourself to the pastries. And let me know if there's anything I can do." He patted his breast pocket to check for his glasses, and then his right trouser pocket for his notes. "I'm off."

Penelope waited until Jake had settled in on the floor next to her, a bear claw on a plate in one hand. "What's first?"

He handed her the plate and pulled a pen and notebook from his back pocket. "I have a list of the six people I know are missing dogs. I talked to Isolde last night, but I'm going to talk to the other five today and see how the dogs got out. Plus, there's a cat missing — I have my doubts that one is connected, but the time fits so I'm going to go talk to those owners, too." He watched her eat a piece of his pastry. "How stale is it?"

Penelope rocked one hand back and forth. "Not exactly fresh, but you won't break a tooth on it either." She handed the plate back to him and leaned on his shoulder to look at what he had written. "What does that say about Isolde? She was yodeling when Guinevere was taken?"

"She was at *yoga*. That's clearly a *G* not a *D*."

Penelope picked up his notebook and extended her arm. "What's that line on the end, then?"

"That's just a line. My pen slipped."

Penelope handed the notebook back. "Too bad. I'd join a yodeling club."

Jake shook his head. "Nope. Not even going to make a comment on that."

"Coward." Penelope squinted at the notebook again. "So she went to yoga at six in the morning, and then straight to the final library garden cleanup, and when she got back home Guinevere was gone."

"That's about it. The door leading to the backyard was open, but she's not completely sure she ever closed it. She had the carpets cleaned the day before and she was trying to air out the house before she had committee members over later in the day." He paused. "Do you need me to move this farther away for you? Or we could get you a little arm extension, sort of like a selfie stick, but for people who refuse to accept their eyes have changed as they've gotten older."

Penelope elbowed him. "You scoff, but we can call it a 'helpy' stick and make millions. And you're throwing stones inside your own glass house." She tore off another piece of his bear claw. "Mostly I just need you to write a little more legibly."

Jake's laughter rang out in the room. "You really want to go there? I thought I was walking a dog named Crabby for a week until I got a look at her tags."

Penelope grinned. That one definitely *had* been her fault. Luckily, Cally's owner found the whole thing hilarious, mostly because the name Crabby fit the dog's personality. "Okay, so Guinevere disappeared sometime between six and eight yesterday morning. Bella also disappeared yesterday morning between seven and eight while Carol was at the garden cleanup. Does Isolde normally go to that yoga class?"

"Good question. The answer is no. She usually goes to the eight o'clock class. *And* she said she'd been planning to skip it completely, but she woke up early and decided at the last minute that she would go to the six o'clock class." He handed her the plate and scribbled an illegible note at the bottom of the page. "It's possible someone was watching her house and saw her leave. Is it common knowledge there are yoga classes that early in the morning?"

Penelope had another bit of the pastry. "I assumed there was at least one studio with classes that early, but I've never checked. If I was awake that early in the morning and wanted to get sweaty and hold weird poses, I'd wake you up and try that one thing again."

He patted her thigh. "Someday that thing is going to knock your socks off."

"I'll hold you to that." She leaned over and kissed his cheek. "But I think what you were trying to ask is whether someone would assume Isolde would go to early morning yoga, and I guess I'd have to say no. Unless she made a habit of it."

"I agree. So it's likely that someone knew both Isolde and Carol would be at the garden cleanup from seven to eight. That narrows things down a little." He stopped and turned his head to look at her squarely. "You're making that face."

"It doesn't actually narrow it down." After a second of thought, she picked up the rest of the bear claw and ate it. Jake could always get up and get another one.

"How many people would have access to the sign-up sheets? It would just be whoever was in charge and anyone else signing up, wouldn't it?" His gaze went down to the empty plate. "I don't even remember eating that thing."

"Weird, isn't it? Maybe the low blood sugar is affecting you. You'd probably better eat another one just to be sure." As he stood up and walked to the pantry, she returned to the original topic. "All the sign-ups are online. Anyone can look at them."

"Anyone?"

Penelope winced. "Anyone. You have to be logged in to edit them, but anyone can view them. Last year they had a bunch of problems with people not knowing where they were supposed to be, and not being able to access the lists to find out, so… they made it easier."

Jake looked like he was getting a headache. "Anyone?" he repeated.

Penelope nodded. "I get that it's kind of a security and privacy issue, but it also means someone like Esther could notice that there were no sign-ups for the booth building team. If she hadn't looked, nobody would have known until Isolde drove by to check on them."

"I know I'm going to regret asking this, but…" Jake paused to pour himself another cup of coffee from the freshly brewed pot. "What else is there besides the volunteers' names? The telephone numbers? The addresses?"

"Oh. I think it's just the name and contact number." Penelope took out her phone and went to the website. "Yes. Just the name and telephone number."

Jake blew out a breath. "So it would still have to be someone who knew people from the gardening club." He walked back over and settled down on the floor again.

"Except…" Penelope kept tapping on her phone.

"Yes?"

"Well, all the houses that are being judged in the contest are listed on another page. So if you have the name, you'd also have the address." She put her phone down next to her leg. "You should probably eat that. It looks like you're getting one of those headaches you get when you wait too long to eat."

"So anyone with internet access would have known which houses were likely to be empty yesterday morning."

"That's the long and short of it, yes."

"Making great progress here." He scratched out something at the bottom of the page and flipped to the next one.

"The other four dogs, plus possibly one cat, were taken Wednesday evening during the meeting."

"Or possibly got out when substandard fencing fell over in the wind."

"Or got out when substandard fencing fell over in the wind," he agreed. "Though I would think they would have been found by now if that were the case."

"Maybe, maybe not. People are weird when they find loose dogs. Most of the time, they bring them to the shelter, or at least take them to their vet to check for a microchip. But there are always the people who wait to see if a poster goes up, or just decide a loose dog has been abandoned and then… keep it." She squinted at his notes. "But probably not all four of them."

"Yeah, I think there's definitely *something* going on. I'm just not sure what." He tapped his pen on the notebook. "Was there a sign-up online for the Wednesday meeting?"

"No."

"Thank god. We might actually be able to shrink the suspect pool from 'everyone with internet access' to something slightly more manageable." He saw her face and sighed. "Or not."

"The meeting was mandatory for everyone whose house was entered in the contest."

Jake flipped his notebook closed. "Excellent. Glad we had this talk. Hopefully, I'll find something linking all the owners when I talk to them."

Penelope rested her head on his shoulder. "CJ's right. There's no money in dog stealing. It's not like pet insurance will pay for ransom."

"And why wait two days before making the ransom calls? I think you're right about the gift card calls coming from someone who saw the poster and decided to make some money." He opened his notebook again and moved to a fresh page. "So if the motive isn't money, what might it be?"

Penelope sipped her coffee and scratched Spot's shoulders while she thought. "Okay, assuming there's a real reason, and this isn't some weirdo who just hates little dogs and the rose garden society..."

"Yes. Start with that assumption."

"I can't come up with a motive, but it seems odd that all the owners are competing in the festival competition."

"Are we really sure about that, though? There could be dogs missing we don't know about. What's the best way to check on that?"

"Talk to someone at the shelter," Penelope answered promptly. "They should have a list."

"I'm going down there when they open this morning to check on the dogs they have, just to make sure. I'll add anyone else I find to the list. Assuming there hasn't been a computer glitch and all these dogs aren't sitting in the shelter, my plan is to talk to the owners after that." He brought up her calendar on his phone. "How about I schedule the interviews starting at 9:30? That will give me time to go to the shelter, and then I can pick you up at the Orson house. You should be done with the holy terror by then, right?"

Penelope grinned. "If you walk ten feet in front of us as we go around the block, we'll definitely be back by then." Smaug Orson was a thirteen-year-old Yorkie with three remaining teeth and one semi-functional eye, but he hated all men with a passion and had been known to hurl himself at moving vehicles to get to the occupants.

"Aren't there rules about using the intern as bait?" Jake reached over to pet Spot, then stood up. "I'm off to the shelter."

Penelope tugged at the hem of his jeans. "Remember. No adopting another dog, no matter how pathetic they are."

"I'll stay strong." Jake grinned and went out the door.

"I'm trusting you!" The door closed as she finished. Penelope sighed and looked at Spot. "Who would steal a dog?"

Spot wagged her tail and grunted.

"Absolutely," Penelope agreed, and rubbed the dog's ear.

CHAPTER 11

*P*enelope was just locking the front door of the Orson house when Jake drove up. "Perfect timing," she called to him.

He rolled down the window. "You're using the key? Where's your commitment to lock picking?"

At the sound of Jake's voice, Smaug launched into a volley of barking inside the house. "Hush, buddy. It's just Jake." Penelope tested the door handle to make sure it really was locked, then jogged to the car and got into the passenger seat. "I need to get faster before I can practice during the day in full view of the neighbors. Who are we going to talk to first?"

"The Smiths. I thought it would be good to start there so we can make sure they aren't being conned out of money again."

Penelope pulled the seatbelt across her chest as Jake accelerated. "I think Jillian put a twenty-four-hour hold on all their credit cards, so they should be safe for a few more hours, but it's probably as good a place to start as any. I take it the dogs weren't at the shelter."

"Nope. They had a pug that looked like a miniature

Brutus, but he was adopted and just waiting to be neutered, so I wasn't even tempted." He grimaced. "Besides, after the whole thing with the pug in our scent tracking class, I'm not bringing one home."

Brutus had graduated from the beginning scent tracking class and now was a proud member of the intermediate class. Unfortunately, his nemesis, a little pug that kept humping everything in sight, had followed. The second time Brutus had urinated on the smaller dog, Jake had paid for the owner to take him to the groomer. It hadn't strictly been Jake's fault — if the pug's owner had been paying attention, the dogs never would have made contact — but Jake decided it was worth it just to calm the waters.

"Did the shelter have any other cases to add?"

He nodded, but didn't take his eyes off the road. "Three possibilities, if they haven't shown up again already. But for privacy reasons, they're going to call the owners and have them get in touch with me if they want me to look into it." His voice was dry. "They aren't all on a website with names, addresses, and phone numbers because it turns out the county understands privacy issues."

Penelope gave him an arch look. "Oh, the rose garden society *understands* privacy issues. They just don't have anyone who knows how to build the website properly, and when they got a quote to hire a professional, everyone just agreed that it didn't matter that much anyhow." She paused to let Jake sigh deeply. "They may have a point. Two seconds online would get all that information."

"Not the lists of who would be at each event."

"Well, no, but it's hard to imagine why anyone would care who can see the lists. Until something like this happens."

"And then it's too late." Jake slowed and pulled to the curb. The Smiths were in their yard, an oasis of perfectly groomed citrus trees, river rocks, stone paths bordered by moss, and a miniature waterfall under a cedar pergola. "Anything I should know before we talk to them?"

Penelope considered. She knew the Smiths through Esther, but she'd never spent much time talking to them. "We should probably talk to them separately. Jillian is the more practical one. If they're together, she's always going to answer the questions even if she has no idea, and Bill will never disagree with her." She shrugged. "But chances are Jillian will have all the useful information anyhow. Bill tends to get sidetracked and start talking about railroads."

"Ah." Jake undid his seatbelt, but didn't otherwise move.

Penelope took pity on him. "I'll take Bill and you can get the facts from Jillian." Watching his profile, she could see his relief. Jake usually preferred talking to people who just came out and said things. Penelope didn't mind verbal detours — she often found out interesting things that way. Plus, she was known for taking the occasional conversational side road herself. But she couldn't resist a little dig at Jake before she opened the car door. "Besides, I'm sure Jillian will want to tell you everything we're doing wrong in our garden."

He glanced over in dismay. "Maybe you should talk to Jillian. I'll be able to keep Bill on topic better."

"Too late. Just blame it all on me and promise to do better next year." Penelope climbed out of the car and ducked to look at him. "Are you coming?"

Separating the Smiths had turned out to be ridiculously easy. They had been doing a mid-day cleanup when Jake and Penelope arrived, with Bill removing leaves from the ground by hand and Jillian walking beside him, pointing them out. As far as Penelope knew, Bill's eyesight was still good, and Jillian was able to stoop just as easily, but she wasn't going to judge; Jillian and Bill had been married for fifty years. Whatever they were doing worked for them.

Penelope pulled Bill away from his wife by the simple expedient of asking to see where their dog, Briar, normally spent her time. Bill promptly dropped his handful of leaves and headed back along the path, beckoning Penelope to follow.

Half an hour later, Penelope and Jake climbed back into the car. Jake stared through the windshield and blinked.

Penelope bit her cheek to hide a smile. "How did it go with Jillian?"

Jake shook his head and started the car. "As far as the dog goes, nothing unexpected. Briar was inside the house when they went to the meeting on Wednesday night. Bill almost stayed home with the dog because of the storm, but Jillian insisted they both go. I gather that's been a point of contention for the last couple days."

Penelope nodded. "I don't think Bill is going to let her forget it anytime soon."

"No, though him falling for the gift card scam is expected to sway the judges. If you believe Jillian." Jake checked over his shoulder before he pulled out into the street.

"Ah, the marriage judges. We should get in on that."

Jake's lips twitched. "I wrote down a list of clubs and other things they are involved in so we can check with everyone else, but it sounds like the rose garden is their main social outlet." He sighed. "Also, we should have planted a different kind of tree, our soil is all wrong, and the mulch on the driveway really ought to be spread soon." He glanced over at Penelope. "It's only been there half a day. How does she know it's there? And how does she even know where we live?"

Penelope rummaged through her backpack until she found her water bottle. "If you think the entire rose garden society hasn't been watching what you've been doing with the yard for the last few months, you're underestimating them."

"Maybe I should have had a sign-up sheet for them to help. Have the newspaper set up an open calendar or something." He glanced over. "How did it go with Bill?"

"Did you know that China and Russia have different train track widths, so when you take a train from one to the other, they lift up the cars with everyone still inside and swap in a different set of wheels? The thing the wheels are attached to are called bogies."

"Uh huh." Jake put his left turn signal on and stopped to

wait for the oncoming traffic to pass. "I take it that means you didn't get anything new about the dog."

"Oh. Actually, I did. I just wanted to tell you about the trains before I forgot, because it was interesting." She took a drink. "First off, Briar has been taking antibiotics for a bladder infection. It's unlikely to cause lasting harm, but I had to talk Bill off the ledge for a while because he's convinced something terrible will happen if she doesn't get her meds right away. Second, Bill and Jillian usually keep two spare keys outside the house — one for the front door under the big planter, and another one for the back door inside the shed in the backyard."

"Of course they do. Why do people even bother having locks on their doors?"

"To give me a chance to practice lock picking. But that's not the interesting part. They *usually* keep both keys outside, but Bill had to use the front door key a week ago when he went on his afternoon walk and Jillian left to buy groceries while he was gone. The marriage judges might need to make a ruling because Bill had expressed an interest in going along and Jillian claims she didn't hear him."

Jake shook his head but kept his eye on traffic.

"Then he forgot the key was in his pocket and it went through the laundry Wednesday afternoon. And because of that, it wasn't in its usual spot Wednesday night."

Jake accelerated into the turn. "Interesting."

"I thought so. I mean, everyone can figure out to look under the planter or the mat, but who knew they kept a back door key in the shed?"

"The shed isn't locked?"

"It is, but the shed key is under the rock right next to the path. I'm pretty sure it's the first place anyone would look. It's certainly the first place *I* would look. The rock seems out of place there."

Jake glanced at an address written in his notebook and parked at the curb. "Did he say who would have known about the key in the shed?"

"He says nobody, but… He showed me the shed and it's on a hook, labeled 'Back Door'."

Jake brightened. "That still narrows it down to people who have been in the shed. There can't be that many."

"Well…" Penelope let her voice trail off.

Jake's scribbling paused. "What?"

"You can see it through the glass on the shed door. And they do a *lot* of tours of their garden. Mostly to the other rose garden society members, but I think they did a few fundraisers there during the last election." She reached over to pat his knee. "Still. It's almost certainly someone who lives here in town. That's a much smaller group than 'anyone who can access the internet'."

Jake gave her a pained look and scratched out what he'd written. "Anything else?"

Penelope looked at the ceiling, trying to remember. She probably ought to have written everything down, but when she tried to write and talk, she made a mess of both. Normally she didn't have trouble remembering conversations, but Bill had kept skipping back to train-related topics, so their talk had been a little disjointed. "Oh! There was one other interesting thing, though I doubt it has anything to do with the dogs. I'm pretty sure Jillian and Bill are judges for the festival this year."

The hand holding his notebook dropped to Jake's leg, but he looked interested. "Really? He let that slip?"

The judging panel for the festival was the town's most closely guarded secret. After the debacle three years prior, when bribery had been uncovered involving at least four different contestants, the committee had decided nobody could bribe the judges if they didn't know who they were.

Thus, the shadow judging panel was born.

In order to be considered as a festival judge, gardeners needed to have been rose garden society members in good standing for at least five years, be willing to view all the competitors during the three days of the festival, and have a solid understanding of the judging criteria. Those potential judges then filled out applications and underwent a preliminary check to ensure their qualifications were acceptable. That part of the judge selection process hadn't changed.

The next part had caused some controversy. The rose garden committee selected the actual judges, but didn't publicize their choices. Actual judges were not allowed to let anyone know they had been selected.

Members who *hadn't* been chosen were asked to continue as if they had been, down to filling out the official judging forms. The wisdom of this had been seen the year before, when Mildred Hoffstedter had broken her hip on the second day of the competition and been hospitalized with five houses left to visit. When her entreaties to the responding paramedics to drive past the remaining houses on the way to the hospital had fallen on deaf ears, the rose garden committee had agreed to select a replacement judge from the non-judges.

Faced with the possibility that a battlefield promotion might occur at any time, everyone who applied to be a judge carefully kept quiet about whether they had been selected. Betting pools and loud arguments resulted, but at least the bribery attempts had been curtailed.

Penelope rocked a hand back and forth. "Not exactly. He started to tell me about why they were delayed on the way home from the Wednesday night meeting, and then mid-sentence he jumped to explaining how train couplers work. Except he'd already explained that to me at Esther's, the last time I talked to him."

Jake looked dubious. "Really? You think you've cracked the code, based on a train enthusiast telling you something that he'd already told you before?"

Penelope tapped his leg. "You laugh, but Bill remembers who he tells things to. He knew that we talked about the weak points of the steam engines at the high school basketball game the year before last. Briar's bed in the kitchen looks like a train car, and he mentioned that the coupler on the end was a little different from the one we'd talked about at Esther's in January."

Jake nodded slowly. "Huh." Then he grinned. "It just occurred to me that I don't have to explain the logic to all that in case notes that someone else is going to look at." He sat up. "So Bill and Jillian are judges?"

"Probably as a couple. Which means it's likely Jillian filling out the form, but I think their gardening opinions are nearly identical. They're organic non-natives with a slight color bent."

Jake nodded, as if that made sense. Because it did.

The rose garden society members fell into factions. The Smiths practiced organic gardening, chose plants based only on whether they were appropriate for the climate and not whether they had historically been grown in the region, and preferred a dash of contrasting color in their garden layouts instead of just different shades of green.

Festival judges were expected to be agnostic when making their choices, but it was generally accepted that organic judges would rather light their scoresheet on fire than award extra points to a contestant using herbicides or pesticides. Similarly, non-organic judges would knock points off for any evidence of pests, even if the infestation was under control and the plants were unharmed.

Members of the rose garden society took their yards very seriously.

Jake stretched his back and settled again. "So if you're right..." He stopped and waited.

Penelope shook herself. "Of course I'm right."

"Little slow there. You feeling okay?" He cleared his throat. "Assuming you're right, we have two dogs missing that are owned by festival judges. Coincidence?" He paused. "I'm struggling to come up with a motive for someone to take the judges' dogs."

"You're also assuming Isolde is one of the judges." Penelope tried to keep a straight face. Of course, Isolde didn't confirm or deny that she was one of the selected judges, but everyone assumed she was. It was such a sure thing that there wasn't even a betting line on it. "But I can't think of a motive either. It might just be one of those weird coincidences." She nodded at the house where they had stopped. "Josie definitely isn't a judge."

Jake looked from the yard back to her. "How do you know?"

She could understand his confusion. Josie's yard had the carefully planned and executed look of someone who took her gardening seriously. Native grasses lined a dry creek bed made of river stones that wended its way under two bridges. Two Adirondack-style chairs made from irregular branches rested in front of a fire pit. The inviting landscape looked effortless, which Penelope was pretty sure meant it was anything but.

"Because she only moved here three years ago." Penelope opened the car door and climbed out. She delivered mail to this address and had yet to figure out what Josie did for a living. It was something that kept her working at home. Penelope had heard the whir of a sewing machine more than once as she put mail through the slot in the door, but she didn't know any tailors that worked out of their own house without a stream of customers showing up or at least a sign.

Jake got out and locked the doors. He slid an arm around her waist as they walked up the path. "You know a *frightening* amount of information about the people who live in this town."

Penelope smiled at him. "Keep giving me compliments like that and who knows what might happen?"

"I have a few suggestions… But work first."

"Spoilsport." Penelope lifted the metal ring to knock on the door, but it opened before she could let it fall.

"Have you found him yet?" Josie always reminded Penelope of an adult acting in a child's show, with her exaggerated movements and way of talking. Today was no exception. Her face fell when she saw their empty arms. "Piggins is dead, isn't he?"

Jake coughed. "There's no evidence of that."

Josie's shoulders drooped. "Sorry. When you said you wanted to come over and talk about him, I thought maybe you'd found him already."

Penelope gestured behind Josie at the house. "Maybe we could come in and talk?"

"Oh! Of course." Josie flung the door wide to expose a large living room with multiple pictures of a little white dog holding an orange stuffed animal in his mouth. "Excuse the mess. I've been worried sick about Piggins. And I have a custom job due in a few days."

Aside from a couch and coffee table, the room held a long table supporting a manikin head encased in a black stocking with a one-inch layer of foam on top. Bits of foam had dropped onto the floor. Scattered on the table were a glue gun, sewing machine, scissors, and more sheets of foam. Multiple clear bins holding wildly colored faux fur were stacked in the corner.

Only as they were heading to the kitchen did Penelope remember she'd never warned Jake about what breed Piggins was. She was fairly certain he had no idea what a Bichon Frise was, and would probably be confident of his identification of Piggins as a poodle.

They followed Josie into a spotless kitchen and wedged themselves around the table in the breakfast nook. Jake put his notebook on the table. "First things first. When did you notice your dog was missing?"

"When I came back on Wednesday night. Normally I wouldn't leave him alone at home, but I knew Isolde would have Guinevere with her, and Piggins hates Guinevere. I didn't want there to be any *more* problems, so I left Piggins at home with his blankey and Mr. Cuddles."

Penelope watched Jake's writing slow and end with three question marks. She decided she might need to take over. Besides, that would keep Jake from calling Piggins a poodle, and Penelope had no desire to sit through the not-a-poodle lecture by another offended Bichon owner. "Mr. Cuddles is his toy?"

"Oh! Yes." Josie jumped out of her seat, skipped into the living room, and came back with a battered orange toy that might have been a carrot when it was new. "Piggins never goes anywhere without Mr. Cuddles. That's why I know he didn't just get out and run away."

"What time did you get back?"

"About nine-thirty. I would have been back sooner, but I was starving. And since Piggins wasn't with me, I decided to get a hamburger and fries. His vet says he needs to stop eating so many fries, so I haven't been going to the drive through as often, but I thought Piggins would never know..." She sniffed.

Jake had written *9:30. Hamburger & fries.* Penelope thought that was a sign she should keep going. Then he underlined the *Hamburger & fries,* and she decided he was probably just getting hungry.

She looked away from the notebook, worried about drawing Josie's attention to Jake's lack of notes. "What happened when you got home?"

"I knew something was wrong right away. Normally Piggins sits in the window waiting for me." She twisted in her seat to point Mr. Cuddles at the living room window. "I thought maybe the wind was bothering him and he was hiding under the bed, but he wasn't there. Then I looked in the master bathroom, figuring he might have gone in there, but..." She continued to list all the rooms in the house where she hadn't found Piggins, not giving Penelope a chance to stem the tide.

Jake scribbled a note that might have been *not in house* and then drew a box around the food order on the line above.

Finally, after Piggins hadn't been found in the kitchen either, Penelope nodded. "And were all the doors locked?"

"Well, no, but then, they weren't when I left either. Everyone around here locks up their houses and then leaves a key in the most obvious place."

Jake and Penelope exchanged a glance.

A look of intense guilt passed over Josie's face. "I always thought there was nothing worth stealing, so why bother locking it all up? But I never thought about someone taking Piggins. What kind of person would take a Bichon Frise?"

Jake's pen stilled and he looked confused. He opened his mouth and Penelope stomped on his foot. When he grunted, she jumped in with another question. "Is Piggins microchipped? Do you have the number?" If the microchip was properly registered, there would be no need to get the number, but with any luck Josie would need to leave the room to get the paperwork.

Josie did get up, but only to dig through one of the

kitchen drawers. "It's in here someplace, along with his AKC papers."

Penelope decided that was as good a chance as she was going to get. As Jake turned to her and mouthed *What?*, she did a quick search on her phone and then handed it over.

Josie found the microchip registration packet and brought it over to the table. As Jake surreptitiously educated himself on the dog breed, Penelope made a show of copying down the microchip number in his notebook.

Jake put Penelope's phone face-down on the table. "Have you noticed anyone new in the area? Maybe watching your house?"

Both Josie and Penelope looked at him.

"With the festival, everyone is staring at all the houses," Penelope said.

Josie nodded vehemently. "And even before that, half the houses have hired people to help out in the last few weeks." She rolled her eyes. "The Washingtons hired Red and his sons to redo the yard and put in stones. If you think it looks bad now, wait a few weeks for when the weeds grow up through the stones. I don't know what they're going to do then."

Penelope glanced out the window toward the house in question. "Probably douse it with weed killer once a week until they hire someone to do it correctly. Since when has Red done landscaping?"

"Technically, he hasn't started yet. I'd call that vandalism, not landscaping. But as far as I know, this is the first time anyone has paid him to do whatever that is." She sighed. "They tried to get me to do it, but their budget wouldn't have even covered the plants, much less the labor. So now I have to look at *that*." Her arm flung out with the last word.

Jake cleared his throat. "Has anyone contacted you about Piggins since he went missing?"

"Yes, but it was just some scammer who knew what I posted online. When I asked what color Piggins had his nails painted, he hung up."

Jake looked confused again, so Penelope preemptively tapped his foot. He pressed his lips together and scribbled *nails painted* on the page. Penelope glanced at Josie's nails, which were red with a line of yellow down the center. "Are they the same as yours?"

"Yes. We did our nails on Monday night."

Jake was staring meditatively at a spot near the ceiling, and Penelope was pretty sure he was trying to imagine painting Brutus's toenails. Brutus did not like having his feet touched.

Penelope took advantage of his reverie to flip back a page. She read off the list of clubs Jillian and Bill belonged to, and wasn't surprised when the only overlap was the rose garden society. The Smiths were in their seventies. Josie was maybe in her thirties, though Penelope found it difficult to accurately guess the ages of people under forty.

After confirming that Josie couldn't think of anyone who had been bothering her, or who had ever suggested they would want to take her dog, Jake flipped his notebook closed and they all stood up.

"If you think of anything else, you have my number," Jake said as they walked through the living room.

Josie nodded. "And if you find out anything at all, please please please let me know. I can borrow money if I need to. My patrons online are really generous if I need something."

Jake looked ready to leave, but Penelope saw her opening to get an answer to the question she'd had for nearly three years. "What is it you do?" She gestured to the worktable.

Josie's chin went up just a fraction. "I make custom fursuits. For furries." Apparently Penelope's reaction passed some test, because her shoulders relaxed slightly. "Do you want to see some of my work?"

"Absolutely!" Penelope glanced at Jake. "I'll explain what furries are later." He put his hands up and took a step back.

Meanwhile, Josie had opened her laptop and brought up a carousel of pictures. Adult sized costumes of blue and silver wolves with wide eyes and plush fur switched to a green and purple owl and then a black and gold wolf in a monk's robe, ears coming through the top of the hood.

Penelope looked at Josie. "You make those? From scratch? Those are *amazing*."

Josie nodded. "I went to design school and spent two years being miserable at a fashion house. Then a friend took me to a furry convention and... my life changed. I also sell just tails and sometimes just the body, but mostly I create the whole fursuit including the head and feet. I'm booked solid for the next six months." She waved an arm at the table. "That's why I'm in here working instead of just driving around trying to find Piggins."

"I don't think Piggins is out on the street, anyhow," Penelope said. She looked back at all the supplies. "And do the people who buy these tell you what color they want, or do you just create something and they're happy with what they get?"

Josie laughed, for the first time since they'd come into the house. "Oh, no! I get a detailed description with the colors and name and gender, plus how long the fur is supposed to be, and if there are any special markings." Her face fell. "This customer has been waiting six months for a dog that looks like Piggins except in purple fur and now..." She looked at the stack of fake fur and sighed.

Penelope turned to go and then froze. "Josie, how does your customer know what Piggins looks like? Are they local?"

"No. He's not even in the country." Josie pointed at the camera linked to her laptop. "I make tutorials for other people who want to make their own. And three times a week I livestream while I'm working so my patrons can watch. Piggins is usually running around while that's going on, so all my subscribers have seen him."

Jake abruptly left his post by the door and came back into the living room. "Anyone with an internet connection could have seen him?"

"Well, anyone who is one of my patrons." Josie looked slightly embarrassed. "People pay money every month for access to the livestreams."

Penelope looked at the pile of foam. There really was a way for artists to support themselves. "But they wouldn't necessarily know where you live, would they?"

"Well… I give my patrons my address. They sometimes send me or Piggins things. Drawings, stuffies, snacks, that sort of thing." She must have seen something in Jake's face, because she crossed her arms over her chest. "I used to worry about stuff like that, but if someone wants your address, they'll find it, no matter what you do. And the only time I ever had a problem with a stalker, it was some loser who kept trying to follow me home from the grocery store." She shrugged and let her arms drop. "Furries may seem kind of weird, but they're usually really nice people."

Penelope looked at her husband. "I somehow doubt the Smiths are furries. So if all the disappearances are related, Josie's patrons aren't involved." She looked back at Josie. "How many people watch those streaming things?" Finding out that it was just a handful of people who didn't live in the area would make Jake feel better.

"It varies. I have about two hundred patrons at various subscription levels, but I don't usually get more than fifty of them on any one livestream. But like I said, if whoever has

Piggins wants money, I can probably raise it if I have enough time."

Penelope blinked.

Jake took her arm and turned her toward the door. He looked over his shoulder to talk to Josie. "Call us if anyone gets in touch about Piggins. I'll let you know what we find."

* * *

PENELOPE MADE IT TO THE CAR IN SILENCE. JAKE GOT BEHIND the steering wheel and then turned to her. "Okay, go ahead."

"Two hundred patrons! With that many people subscribing, they don't even need to be paying that much every month to have the entire mortgage payment covered. What an amazing business model!"

"Two hundred strangers staring at her three times every week."

"True. Did you see those costumes she creates, though? That's art. If I tried to get that many people paying to watch me, I'd probably have to get naked." She thought about it. "Or maybe just show my feet. There are a surprising number of people really into feet."

Jake rubbed at his forehead. "I think we may be getting a little off track. Did we learn anything new here?"

"We learned that whoever took her dog probably went through the unlocked front door and hasn't tried to contact her yet. And *you* learned that a Bichon Frise is different from a poodle, and also you learned about furries."

Jake stared at his notebook and nodded. "That pretty much covers it."

"And *I* learned that you're going to sneak off to get a hamburger and fries while I'm walking dogs."

Jake laughed and flipped his notebook closed. "I was

thinking a cheeseburger and fries, but you caught me. Do you want me to bring you something?"

"Only if you love me." Penelope looked at her schedule. "Who's next? I may have to leave you on your own so I can go take care of some clients."

"I told Carol Entweiler I'd be by to talk to her in about fifteen minutes."

"Perfect. I've already talked to her, so I'll let you go see if there are any new connections. Then you can call me when you're ready for the next one and I'll see if I can make it."

Jake nodded and started the car. "Where should I drop you off?"

"Second and Dahlia. I promised Lorri I'd help her bathe Tiny since he got booted from the groomer."

"Lucky you."

They were only a few blocks away. Penelope spent the time thinking about the missing dogs. "Do you think they're alright?"

"The dogs?" Jake glanced over to check. "Yes."

Something in her relaxed at hearing him say it so confidently. "Why?"

"Because the type of person who would hurt the dogs is also the type of person who would want to make sure the owners knew about it. Ergo, it isn't about hurting the dogs. Whoever has them wants something else. We just haven't figured out what it is yet." He pulled up to the curb. "We'll get there." He raised her hand to kiss her palm. "I'll call you before I get in line to order."

Penelope got out of the car and watched him drive away. Then she turned and headed inside to help bathe a Rottweiler who was afraid of water.

CHAPTER 13

The noon bells had already finished chiming by the time Penelope made it to the park where she had promised to meet Jake. For a moment, she didn't see him, but then she saw Brutus standing on top of a person prone on the grass. If that person wasn't Jake, she was going to need to apologize quickly.

She had only walked halfway across the grass when Brutus saw her. The mastiff jumped onto the ground and ran toward her, leaving Jake curled up in a fetal position. At least Jake was aware enough of who was coming to drop the leash, so he didn't get dragged.

Penelope turned to the side when Brutus ran up. He sat and she gave him a treat after she picked up the leash. "You better not have hurt Jake," she said as she scratched his ears. He leaned against her. They walked the rest of the way. "You okay there, Scrappy?"

With a groan, Jake climbed to his feet. "His paws need to be registered as a deadly weapon." He scooped up the fast food bag. "It was rough, but I protected your lunch from a vicious beast intent on stealing it."

"That's weird." Penelope sat down on the grass. "From over there it looked like you were playing with the dog." She took the bag from him, opened the top, and inhaled deeply. "That's the stuff." She dug out the burger labeled extra cheese and handed it to him. "Anything new from Carol?"

"It looks like the rose garden society is the common link so far. But they've also all gone to the dog park at least once in the last few months."

"Is there anyone in town who hasn't?" Penelope unwrapped the kid's burger and gave it to Brutus, took out her own cheeseburger, and then tore open the bag so she and Jake could share the fries. "None of them are regulars."

"No, but it occurred to me if someone saw them at the dog park, they would know who had small dogs." Jake paused to take a bite.

"True." Penelope thought about it for a minute as she watched Brutus trying to creep closer to the fries without breaking his down-stay. "Does it mean anything that they are all small dogs?"

"Cheaper to feed," Jake answered promptly. "And maybe easier to deal with?" He looked at Brutus. "Though I'd take the big lug over that little shark Smaug any day."

"Smaug just doesn't trust men. It's perfectly understand-able." Penelope tossed a burned fry to Brutus. "But you could toss a towel over Smaug and grab him if you needed to. Most people would throw out their back if they tried to pick up a mastiff. Plus, you can get a small dog crate cheap, or even free, if you look around. Even if you only had a tiny house, you could line up a bunch of crates in one room. Maybe it's just a logistics problem."

"Which brings us right back to the question of why anyone would want to steal a bunch of dogs in the first place." Jake sighed. "I have to admit, I don't have an answer for that yet."

"Could be worse. You could have people pressuring you to find out who is torching random cars."

"Good point."

They watched clouds drift by. Brutus oozed forward.

"Maybe it really is someone holding the dogs for ransom. I guess it *could* be the gift card person." Penelope sat up straighter. "You could run a honey pot."

Jake opened his mouth, then closed it, and finally cleared his throat. "I'm *not* having sex with someone to get these dogs back."

"I may have the wrong name for it." Penelope glanced at him. "But I'm glad to hear that." She ate the last French fry. "Forget the sex part. Maybe we could rule out the person demanding gift cards by putting up our own posters. If they call, then worst case we know for sure they're just getting info from the poster, and best case we can figure out who it is and make them stop."

"And if they don't call…"

"If they don't call, then maybe we take their claim to have the dogs a little more seriously."

"Hm." Jake balled up the empty wrappers and lobbed them into the nearby trash can. "Ha! Did you see that? Didn't even hit the rim."

Penelope patted his shoulder. "Very nice. You're going to crush the three-point contest this year."

"Anyhow, I think the term you're looking for is entrapment, but since we don't really care about the legal case, I suppose it doesn't matter." He got to his feet and reached down to help her up, keeping her hand in his after she'd stood. "I doubt it's going to help find the dogs, but at least it would let me tell Isolde that we're doing *something*. Without stretching the truth so far it's going to bounce back and hurt me."

Penelope let Jake guide her toward the street where he

had parked. "Where to next? We should have time for at least one more before we have to work in the beer tent."

"Time to talk to the cat people." He frowned. "No, wait. That makes it sound like I'm talking about those furries. Time to talk to the people whose cat went missing the night of the storm. I'm pretty sure it's unrelated, but it's not like there are so many clues we can just ignore some before we've checked them out."

"Are we stopping by the house to drop off the big lug first?"

"Nope." Jake smiled. "The big lug is my secret weapon."

Natalie and Rachel Devlin-Koning might have had the case that didn't fit, but that didn't mean they weren't just as worried.

"I thought I'd be home long before the storm began, so I left the windows open in the morning," Rachel said. She was slouched in the chair across from them in a t-shirt, shorts, and bare feet, and had the look of someone who had worked so many odd hours lately that she wasn't sure if she was supposed to be awake or asleep. "But then I ended up working a double shift at the hospital and didn't make it home until almost midnight. Nat was still at her dad's house until yesterday. I thought Blur had just knocked out the screen and gone through the opening. She did that once before, but last time she just sat by the front door meowing to come in."

Natalie picked at her fingernail. "She's an inside cat. We thought she must have gotten scared by the storm and was hiding, but she would have come out by now, right? She's microchipped and I've checked the shelter... Then we heard about all the dogs that were missing."

Jake scribbled a note and looked at Rachel. "Was the house still locked up when you came home?"

Rachel nodded. "Yes. I remember, because I thought Nat might have come home early, so I checked the knob before I put everything down to find my keys."

"Do you keep a key outside?"

Rachel and Natalie exchanged a look. "Not anymore," Natalie replied.

"We used to keep on under the mat, but then some..." Rachel edited the word she was going to use. "Some *guy* kept coming onto the porch and stealing our pride flags and leaving notes in the mailbox. The usual stupid stuff. But we decided to be a little more careful about keeping things locked up."

Jake looked up from his notes. "Did it ever go any further than that?"

Rachel shook her head and yawned widely, belatedly covering her mouth with her hand. "Sorry. No, it was just some notes and the flags."

The kettle whistled. Natalie got up and started adding scoops of coffee to a French press. "I took a bunch of pictures of him standing on our porch one day and threatened to make him famous if he didn't leave us alone." She took the kettle off the stove and poured the boiling water into the press, then stirred the mixture with a metal spoon. "I parked my car in the garage that day, so he thought there was nobody home." Coffee grounds swirled as she carried the press over to the table. "But I'm pretty sure he went back to college. I certainly haven't seen him around at all in the past six months."

"Which is a long way of saying no, we don't keep a key outside," Rachel finished.

"And nothing else was missing when you got home Wednesday night?"

Rachel shook her head. "No."

Natalie laughed once as she brought over four mugs and sat down again. She looked at Rachel. "As if you would notice if someone came in and cleared out the entire house." Her rebuke was good-natured. She turned back to Jake. "But *I* would, and as far as I can tell, everything is still here. Even my grandmother's ugly jewelry."

Rachel blew out a breath. "We'll keep trying. I'm sure someone will steal it someday."

Natalie smiled at Penelope. "Grandma claimed to be psychic. She always told me she'd seen me wearing her jewelry on my wedding day. And then she'd go on and on about how I'd find a doctor and he would be a wonderful husband. Even when I was six, I could have told her *that* was never going to happen, but she was still introducing me to all the unmarried male doctors on the ward every time I visited until the day she died." She reached over and briefly clasped Rachel's hand. "It worked out, though. Her cardiologist introduced me to Rachel."

"And you pinned that brooch-thing inside your dress at our wedding, so… Aside from the husband part, it all came true."

Natalie shrugged. "Sometimes you have to pick and choose the right parts of prophecies to make them work out." She busied herself with the French press.

Penelope nodded. "That's the smartest thing I've heard anyone say in days."

Jake looked around the room. "You said you found a spot where you think Blur got out?"

Rachel stood up. "Here, I'll show you." Penelope and Jake followed her out of the kitchen to the living room overlooking a barren backyard. She pointed to a small window up near the ceiling, next to a hutch that contained stereo equipment and a collection of tiny oil paintings. At the very top of the furniture was a cat bed. "Blur likes to sit up there and watch the birds in the yard. I left that window open when I went to work. It's too small and too high off the ground for someone to use to get into the house."

Penelope sized it up. She might be able to get through it, assuming someone boosted her up to that level, but it would be easier to break some other window. There wasn't an alarm system.

Jake looked like he was making the same calculations. "And the screen had been knocked out?"

"One corner was hanging off. Like I said, I assumed Blur got out on her own. But it's been three days and nobody has seen her and all those dogs disappeared at the same time."

They headed back to the kitchen, where Natalie was pouring coffee.

Penelope accepted a mug, took a sip, and looked at the picture of Blur on the table. The photographer had caught him mid-stretch, his fluffy black coat making him look twice his size. "I have a hard time linking Blur's disappearance to the dogs."

Jake nodded. "I agree." He looked at the other two women. "Obviously, if we find Blur with the dogs, we'll let you know. But there are enough differences that I don't think we will. Aside from Blur being the only cat, the other owners are all members of the rose garden society. You never have been, right?"

Rachel shook her head. "No. We hire a crew to come over once a week and keep everything tidy, but neither of us is into gardening. My thumb is so black I can kill plants by glancing at them." She looked apologetic. "I'm so sorry to waste your time. It's just that we've run out of places to look."

Jake waved off her words. "It was worth the trip just for this coffee. But there is one thing I'd like to try, if you don't mind." He paused and looked almost embarrassed. "I have no idea if this will work. But assuming Blur went out the window under her own steam, I'd like to see if our dog can follow her trail. Maybe she's stuck in a tree, or in someone's garage."

Rachel and Natalie looked at each other. "Go for it," Rachel said. "If it doesn't work, I don't see how we're any worse off."

"Good. You haven't washed the bed next to the window since Blur left, have you?" Jake took another gulp of coffee and looked at Penelope. "Can you get Brutus out and bring him into the backyard? His training leash is in the back. I'll get the bed and meet you back there."

Penelope went outside and down the walkway. Jake had parked in the shade and left all the windows open because nobody would be stupid enough to steal from a car with a gigantic dog inside. She could hear Brutus snoring from ten feet away, but as she walked closer, he scrambled up and poked his head out the window. "Hey, buddy, you ready to do some work?"

Between getting his training leash and treats out of the back, and unhooking his car harness, it took a few minutes to bring Brutus into the backyard. Jake was already waiting with the bagged cat bed in one hand. Rachel and Natalie were watching from inside the house.

Penelope clipped on the leash Jake had been using at class, and Brutus's whole attitude changed. Gone was the goofy dog who just wanted to slobber all over strangers. He knew the leash meant it was time to play the game of finding scents, and, more importantly, a chance to get the good treats. Penelope handed the treats and leash to Jake and stepped back. "Fingers crossed."

Jake opened the bag and held the cat bed out so Brutus could smell. "Brutus! Find it!" As soon as the dog lifted his nose from the bag, Jake closed it back up and tossed the bag to Penelope. "Find it!"

Brutus ran over to Penelope and sat down.

Jake grimaced even as he gave the dog a treat. "I didn't think that one through very well, did I?"

"Let me take this elsewhere so you can try again." Penelope jogged around to the front of the house, opened the door, and put the bed inside. "We're just getting rid of a distraction," she said when Rachel came forward to see what she was doing. She jumped off the porch and ran to the far end of the backyard. "Try now."

Jake started Brutus under the window again. "Find it!"

This time Brutus started sniffing the bushes next to the house, and led Jake around the house, up the steps, and sat down two feet to the side of the front door. Jake looked back at Penelope. "Is he following the path you just took with the bed?"

"Maybe?" She looked at where the dog was sitting. "But maybe not. He's farther over than I would expect if that were the case. They said last time Blur got out she sat on the front porch, right? Maybe she did the same thing for a while this time."

Jake left the leash loose. "Find it!"

After a few glances up at Jake, Brutus walked down the stairs and headed across the front lawn to a clump of bushes and then on to the next lawn. Penelope trailed behind.

Rachel and Natalie came up behind her. "Is it working?" Rachel was still barefoot, with her mug of coffee gripped tightly in one hand.

Penelope took a deep breath while she tried to figure out the answer, then blew it out again. "I'm not sure. Maybe." She watched Brutus trample someone's begonias. "I don't want to get your hopes up too high, but this isn't how he normally detours if he's on a walk. I think he might at least be trailing *a* cat."

Natalie hummed. "But maybe not the *right* cat."

"Exactly."

They were three houses away now. Aside from the begonias, Brutus had crushed part of an herb bed and pushed his way through a privet hedge. Jake had tried to push the branches back together, but it still left a gap. Penelope hoped nobody on the block had been planning on taking any prizes in the festival contest.

At the fourth house, Brutus climbed up the steps and sat down in front of the door. Jake looked over at Penelope. She shrugged.

Natalie looked between Brutus and Penelope. "What does that mean?"

"Well, sitting down is his cue that he found the thing, so he might be saying that the cat came here." She grimaced. "It's also possible he just decided to sit down. Brutus is near the top of his class, but it's only the intermediate class." She didn't add that there were only four dogs in the class, so technically, he was near the bottom of the class as well.

At least he wasn't as bad as the pug.

"We're just grateful you tried," Natalie said.

While Jake and Penelope were staring at each other, trying to figure out what to do next, the door behind Jake opened. Brutus dashed inside, but had barely cleared the lintel when a cat howled. Then Brutus was running backward, whining, with a black cat attached to his face. In his rush, he knocked over Jake. Jake went down on his back and the dog's rear hit the railing on the porch.

Rachel sprinted across the grass, coffee splashing wildly. "Blur! Oh my god, Blur!"

Penelope ran after her.

Over the noise of a grey-haired man in the doorway

yelling, a dog whining, and a cat howling, Penelope heard wood splintering. Rachel tripped and went down. The porch railing was no match for a huge dog trying to reverse away from an attack. Penelope hurdled up the steps just in time to put an arm around Brutus's backside. The railing fell into the annuals below.

Not knowing what else to do, Penelope kept pushing, stepping over Jake in the process. She shoved the dog — and the cat attached to his face — into the house. Then she kicked the door closed behind her.

She found herself in a living room decorated in a cowboy western style, with wagon wheels propping up couch ends, and branding irons on the wall. Penelope grabbed the black and white faux cowhide blanket off the back of the couch and wrapped it around the still-screaming cat and tugged. The cat let go of Brutus and flipped over in the blanket.

With the wriggling and screaming bundle in her arms, Penelope ran for the hallway. The second door on the left turned out to be the bathroom. She crouched, slid the cat and blanket across the tile floor, and yanked the door shut.

Then she took a deep breath and exhaled. A quick check of her hands and arms showed no sign that cat teeth or claws had made it through the blanket.

Brutus cowered by the door, shivering. "I'm sorry, buddy, that wasn't what you expected, was it?" She dug a treat out of her pocket and gave it to him, ignoring the pounding on the door. Then she checked his face.

From all the noise he'd been making, she'd assumed he'd lost an eye, but she found one drop of blood on his ear, and that was the extent of the physical damage. "You're such a good boy." She fed him a couple more treats and picked up his leash. "Let's move you away from the door." This time the treats got her a tail wag. "Okay, I guess we shouldn't put this off any longer."

The door had automatically locked when she'd closed it, and it took her a moment to figure out how to get it open again. When she did, all four people ran inside.

Jake looked reassured by the lack of blood on her. He crouched by Brutus and checked his face. Penelope held up a hand when Rachel and Natalie looked around the room. "The cat is in the bathroom, but I'm pretty sure anyone who goes in there in the next half hour is going to end up in the hospital. Let's just let her calm down a little."

The last person to come in was the man who had opened the door. He tottered over the threshold and grabbed a putter from the umbrella stand next to the door. "If you lot don't leave now, I won't be responsible for the consequences." He raised the golf club, hitting a horseshoe on the wall. It fell to the floor with a clang.

Penelope suppressed a giggle. If she started laughing now, she wouldn't be able to stop.

Rachel still looked like she might ignore Penelope's warning and head into the bathroom. "You have our cat. Blur."

"What? I most certainly do not. That's my cat, Geordie. I've had him ten years."

Rachel shook her head. "No. I know my cat. That was Blur. I'd recognize that sound she was making anywhere."

Natalie nodded. "She makes that sound when she sees strange cats outside."

"You people need to leave. Right now."

Rachel crossed her arms. "Not without my cat."

"He's not your cat!"

Jake had apparently decided an octogenarian with a golf club was not an immediate threat, and was tapping on his phone. That left Penelope to play referee. She crossed her forearms in front of her body. "Time out!"

The three people arguing about the cat stopped talking and looked at her.

Jake looked up and whispered, "That's the sign for an incomplete pass. Timeout is over your head."

Penelope let her arms drop. "Can we start over?" She smiled at the man. "Hi. I'm Penelope Standing. I'm sorry for barging into your house like that, but I really didn't want the cat to run off outside." She completed the introductions.

The golf club lowered a few inches. "John Smith."

"So. Rachel and Natalie's cat, Blur, disappeared a few nights ago, and Brutus tracked her scent here." She held up one finger when John and Rachel opened their mouths to speak. "It sounds like there's a really easy way to tell if this is Blur or Geordie. I heard you call Geordie 'he', right?" After John nodded, Penelope looked at Rachel. "And Blur is female?"

"Yes."

"Great. Then we can figure this out. Just as soon as the cat in the bathroom calms down enough not to kill anyone who touches them."

Jake waved his phone. "There's a *male* black cat that was brought into the shelter Wednesday morning."

The golf club lowered completely. "Geordie got out Tuesday morning when I was bringing my groceries in. He does that every once in a while. So I left his food on the porch. He was sitting there eating when I opened the door after the storm. But... You're saying that wasn't Geordie."

Natalie walked into the living room from the hallway. Penelope hadn't even noticed her leaving. "That's definitely Blur in the bathroom. She has the little white patch on her elbow and everything."

While the three cat owners were apologizing to each other, Penelope nudged Jake. "I think we should take Brutus home before someone lets Blur out of the bathroom."

By the time they left, Natalie was making a list of things she would need from the hardware store to fix the broken railing. Jake's help was waved off. "You found Blur, and that's the important thing." Rachel and John were getting ready to go to the shelter together. For his part, Brutus walked down the porch steps, did a full body shake, and then trotted happily toward the car.

Jake and Penelope followed behind in silence.

Jake sighed. "On the one hand, we successfully tracked a missing cat."

"You should be proud."

"But on the other hand, my giant dog just got beat up by a tiny cat. It wasn't even close. She wiped the floor with him. It's a little embarrassing."

Penelope patted his arm. "He's a lover, not a fighter. Besides, it could have been worse. She probably would have killed the pug if she grabbed his face like that."

Jake brightened. "That's true." He put an arm around her waist. "We have the best dog."

CHAPTER 15

*D*ropping off the best dog at home had taken less than a minute. Brutus had been snoring on the sofa before they'd even made it out the door, apparently not too traumatized by his encounter with the cat.

Since it was a fundraiser, the rose garden festival sold beer under a huge portable tent that took up a few dozen parking spaces. Two lines of caution tape wrapped around the frame funneled people to the entrance where IDs were checked, and there were enough volunteers manning the tent to make sure nobody left with a drink or passed one to someone waiting outside.

Given the number of bars selling better quality beer within easy walking distance, Penelope was surprised the beer tent made money, but Esther insisted it was the highest earner during the weekend.

Passing between the carnival booths on the way there, Jake halted mid-stride to avoid someone attempting the ring toss from a running start. "I still don't understand how he could have the wrong cat for three days and not notice."

"That's because you've never been accused of swapping in

another cat while the owners are on vacation. Cats are famous for changing all their habits at the drop of a hat. An indoor cat that spends a day or two outside is going to act weird afterward." She glanced from a passing child to the water gun booth.

It appeared someone had topped up the supply of prizes by splitting up bulk packs of markers from the stationery store. Penelope hoped they were water soluble, since the smaller children had used them to draw on the only thing available — their own skin and clothes.

Jake sighed. "I'm going to have to spend all my time here avoiding Isolde so she won't ask for an update."

"See? Yet another problem with working the beer tent."

Penelope had *wanted* to volunteer as a tour guide on one of the neighborhood garden walks, but apparently her complete ignorance of plants coupled with her inability to stick to a script disqualified her. So she and Jake had been volunteered for a spot in the beer tent instead.

She grumbled as they walked through the row of games toward the tent. "Where's the fun in listening to someone read a list of plants?" They passed a bored man sitting in the deserted fish pond booth.

"To be fair, most people go on those tours because they're interested in the plants."

"Bah. It's either a rose, or some long grassy thing, or a tree. What else do you need to know? Meanwhile, I could tell people the name of every dog that lived in the neighborhood, and three cute stories about each one. People would be lining up to come on my tour."

Jake glanced at her. "Three cute stories about Smaug. Go."

Penelope smiled. "Smaug is the reason this town has an all-women landscaping company, you know."

"I learn new things every day."

"Yeah, they don't do many houses because they all have other jobs, but Smaug was the inspiration."

"One down, two to go."

"Smaug once jumped out of a moving car to protect a woman being harassed by a man on a bicycle." Penelope shrugged. "Then three teeth fell out when he tried to bite the bicycle tire, but it's the thought that counts."

Jake looked pained. "I'm not sure that story qualifies as cute, but I'll give it to you. One more."

"In all his life, Smaug has only liked one man. He's a gigantic biker who stopped to help Smaug's owner change a tire. He sometimes takes Smaug out for the day in his sidecar."

Jake eyed her suspiciously. "You're making that up."

Penelope held up one hand. "I swear. I have pictures."

They had reached the beer tent. Jake held up the tape for her to duck under. "I'm sold. I'll lobby next year's committee to add the dog facts tour to the schedule. Are there any dog lovers in the frontrunners for the committee spot?"

"That's a good thought. I'm going out with Esther later to scout the competition. Maybe I can put my thumb on the scales…"

Jake smiled. "I've seen you in the garden. You probably want to just leave it to chance."

Iain Hotz had the volunteer sign-in sheet. "Welcome!" He lowered his voice. "I was beginning to think I was going to be trapped here with just a bunch of my students to help. Every professor's nightmare…"

Penelope looked around while Jake had the clipboard. There *did* seem to be a higher ratio of younger women volunteering in the beer tent than elsewhere at the festival, though that could have also been because it was the beer tent. The only other volunteer above thirty was Linnea Kowalcik, still in flip-flops, a halter top, and shorts. Penelope hoped Linnea and Iain weren't going to bring their never-ending arguments from the dog park into the volunteer realm. "What do you need us to do?"

He looked at the clipboard. "Jake? I'll have you help serve behind the counter. And Penny?"

"Penelope."

"Oh, right, sorry. If you could help the other girls keep the area clean, that would be great."

Jake looked ready to tackle her to keep her out of trouble, but Iain's words didn't bother Penelope in the slightest. He'd insulted her twice in a row, getting her name wrong even as he read it from the sign-in sheet, and then using casually sexist language. That *had* to be deliberate.

Penelope had met his type before. She would bet everything she owned he did something similar to all the women in his classes. Most would laugh it off, but there would always be a few that would be inspired to figure out how to gain his approval. Penelope suspected she wouldn't have to dig too hard to find rumors he had dated some of his students.

She gave a smile that bared her teeth. "Sure. Why not? I prefer moving around anyhow." And if she listened to what his students said about him and passed anything troubling along to the appropriate people, well, he'd set it all in motion himself. Jake would have the harder role of being polite to the man for the next two hours.

"Be sure to keep an eye out for anyone trying to sneak into the tent without showing ID."

Penelope grabbed a fresh towel from the stack and moved into the crowd. A few years back, one of the older men on the planning committee had suggested having the volunteers in the beer tent wear dirndls, the traditional Bavarian dresses shown on a certain brand of beer bottles. Esther had raised her hand and asked if the men would really be comfortable wearing skirts like that. The ensuing chaos had derailed the suggestion.

Now Penelope wondered if dirndls were waterproof, because after twenty minutes she'd had more beer sloshed on her than she'd spilled in the last twenty years. It was a warm day, and the beer was cold. Plus, the tent provided one of the few spots of shade, so people came in to sit down and didn't rush to leave. Penelope gathered abandoned cups in one hand and wiped puddled beer off the tables with the other while she thought about the missing dogs.

Whoever had taken the dogs could have found addresses and membership lists online, but they wouldn't have known for sure who would be at the Wednesday night meeting without seeing who showed up. Concerns about the storm meant some people had abandoned the mandatory meeting and the competition in favor of staying home.

The unknown person could have just gone to target houses and knocked to see if anyone was there, but they would risk being remembered if someone actually *did* answer the door. Checking the rose garden meeting parking lot would have worked, but only if they knew the owner of each car. Given how many people drove the same three popular cars, that would be difficult. And a lot of people carpooled or just ignored the weather and walked. Plus, only one person from the household *had* to be there. It wouldn't be obvious from the parking lot if spouses or other members of the family had come along.

The easiest way to see which houses would be empty would be to go to the meeting and then duck out when nobody was looking.

She took another stack of plastic cups to the recycling bag, inconveniently stored at the back of the tent. Luckily, the location meant she could stop by the spot in the corner where Jake was filling cups from the keg.

He looked up. "I'm definitely voting for the dog facts tour next year."

"By then you may have enough stories to be a guide on your own." She dropped the cups into the bag. "Has anyone given you a list of all the people at the meeting?" With a glance around to make sure nobody was close enough to overhear, she explained her reasoning.

Jake put a filled cup on the tray. "I took pictures of the sign-in sheet from the meeting." He took out his phone and sent her the images. "How is it going out there?"

"Definitely not as fun as the dog facts tour would have been, but I can last another two hours."

"That's the spirit." He picked up the tray. "Just give me a signal if you're planning to kill that Iain guy so I can make sure I'm looking the other way."

Penelope leaned forward to kiss his cheek. "That's just one of the benefits of being married. You can't be forced to testify against me."

He grinned. "You know, for some couples that wouldn't be in the top ten."

"If that's in our top ten, I need to try a little harder."

His smile widened. "If you try any harder, I may end up in the hospital."

Penelope watched him walk to the register with the tray, then shook herself out of her reverie to look at the images he'd sent her. Most of the names were ones she'd expected to see. Esther was third, and Josie was in the middle of the second page. Of course Iain was on there — he probably sipped scotch and trimmed roses in a tweed coat with elbow patches.

Both Linnea and her husband, Tom, were on the third page. From the way Linnea had talked about gardening at the dog park, Penelope was a little surprised she had both gone to the meeting and taken volunteer shifts. The contestants were required to volunteer for at least two three-hour blocks. Esther had been responsible for getting Penelope and Jake signed up for even more.

Penelope shoved her phone back in her pocket as Jake returned with an empty tray. "You get to ask Iain about anyone who might have left the Wednesday meeting early. I'll take Linnea."

"Aye aye, captain."

Penelope started wiping down a group of tables near Linnea. "Didn't you say Tom was the gardener? Is he here somewhere?" Linnea's husband wasn't in the group of men handling the customers.

"He's at his mother's." Linnea rolled her eyes. "But at least this gives me a great excuse to avoid going with him. I'd rather volunteer to clean up beer than deal with her."

"How much longer are you stuck here?"

"I stupidly signed up for two shifts in a row, and only found out Professor Useless over there was in charge after I got here." Linnea emptied the liquid at the bottom of the cups into the boxwood bordering the parking lot. "If I'd known I was going to have to spend six hours watching his students sigh and flutter their eyelashes at him, I'd have signed up for the cleanup crew instead."

Penelope wiped the table and followed her to the next spot. "You sound like you know him from more than the dog park."

Linnea glared across the room to where Iain was taking money from customers. "If I wanted to go back and get my degree, I had to finish my prereqs. I thought the fairy tale literature class would be an easy way to get the English requirement out of the way. Turned out to be seven essays in ten weeks, and if there were any typos, you had to resubmit or you didn't get any credit at all." She laughed. "Really, the whole thing was just ten weeks of him talking about how each fairy tale was a metaphor for sex."

"Why am I not surprised?"

"Once I figured that out, I just picked a different kink for each paper and made up some connection to one of the fairy tales. Tom nearly had a heart attack when he saw the one I'd done on bondage and Pinocchio."

Penelope blinked. "There's bondage in Pinocchio?"

Linnea snorted. "Of course not. But it was an easy five pages, and I got the highest grade in the class."

Penelope picked up more cups. "The last time I took a class on literature, I had to read *Moby Dick*. I might have done better discussing fairy tales." She shook her head and changed the subject. "You were at the meeting on Wednesday night, right?"

"Yep."

"Did you notice anyone leaving early? The sign-in sheet has the time people got there, but not the time they left."

Linnea raised one eyebrow. "Don't tell me they're trying to disqualify people from the contest for leaving during the meeting."

"What? No. Nothing like that." Penelope followed Linnea to the next table. "Isolde asked Jake to look into the missing dogs. I was just wondering if there was someone who was gone for a while."

Linnea's eyes flicked over to the men at the front of the tent. "Really? I didn't know he did that sort of thing. But as far as anyone leaving early..." She stared up at the corner of the tent as she thought. "Tom and I were there the whole time, and sadly, I can give Iain an alibi as well. He was behind me, being irritating until the end. As far as everyone else... One of the old men fell over in his chair, and there was a couple minutes of panic when people thought he'd died, but it turned out he'd just fallen asleep. I guess someone could have left then, but I didn't notice it. The problem is they didn't have enough chairs, so people were wandering around at the back and some people stood up and others took their seats."

She shrugged and looked back at Penelope. "Sorry. That's not very helpful, I know. I'll ask Tom when he gets home tonight. Maybe he noticed something." She headed to the recycling area, the click of her flip-flops hitting her heels just audible over the sound of people talking.

Penelope kept wiping tables as she thought. A teenaged boy ducked under the tape, and she stared at him, eyebrows raised, until he gave an embarrassed grin and left again.

Why would anyone take a bunch of dogs? Penelope had been hired by a few clients who had been worried about ex-partners stealing their pets, but that motive fell apart when she looked at this group. Josie, for example, hadn't even dated anyone since she'd had Piggins. And if either Jillian or Bill had a jilted lover waiting in the wings, Penelope would be shocked. Not because of their age, but because they were so rarely apart.

It *had* to come down to money.

Penelope pulled out her phone to check the hours on the closest copying center. It was past time to find out if the gift card caller was involved.

CHAPTER 16

By the time their volunteer shift was over, Penelope had designed a lost dog flier on her phone. It helped that she already had the template she used when clients called.

Jake looked it over as they walked back to the car. "Reward. Missing Chihuahua. Diogy..." He paused and laughed. "Is that *supposed* to be like D-O-G?"

"Yes." Penelope was holding the hem of her shirt and flapping it as they walked, hoping the beer would dry before they got into the car so it didn't soak into the seats. "I've met at least three people who named their dog some variation on that."

"Really? Okay. Tan with three white feet. Pink sparkle collar." He scrolled. "Where did you get that picture?"

"From my phone. That dog belongs to one of Seth's neighbors. I doubt anyone around here would recognize him. The dog, not Seth. Plenty of people would recognize Seth." Her son had grown up here and still came back on a regular basis to visit.

"Got it. Missed by his family. Reward. No questions

asked." Jake stopped walking. "Hang on. That's *my* phone number. We aren't putting up fliers all over town with my phone number on them."

"I can't very well use *my* number," Penelope said. "One quick search will bring up the dog walking business, and then to the marriage announcement, and then all the times you were listed in the paper as acting police chief." Given the way information lingered online, she doubted it would be obvious to a casual searcher that Jake had retired. The whole thing would look like a poorly disguised attempt to hide police involvement. She took a small step in the direction of the car.

He settled more firmly in place. "So you want to give them my phone number directly?"

"Yes. But since nothing links your phone number back to you, it will be fine."

"Except then my phone number will be out on telephone poles and who knows where else and I'll be getting random calls forever." He handed her phone back to her and took out his own. After a few moments of tapping, he looked up. "Use this one instead." He read out a number. Penelope added it to the flier, then called it.

Jake's phone rang.

Penelope disconnected the call. "How did you do that?"

"I signed up for a free number and set it up to forward to my phone. I'll get rid of it as soon as we're done with this. That way I won't be getting calls about a Chihuahua someone might have seen for the rest of my life."

"Clever." Penelope saved the flier and sent it off to the copy center. "If their website isn't lying, we should be able to pick up the copies in twenty minutes. Then you can go move mulch around for a while, and I'll put up fliers. I promised Esther I'd go look at gardens with her this afternoon, anyhow. I can put fliers up along the way."

"You sure you don't want me to put up fliers instead?"

Penelope glanced at him with a bright smile. "I'm not the one who did the math and decided we needed six yards. We can't *both* avoid the mulch pile, or it's still going to be taking up space in the driveway months from now."

"Math doesn't lie."

Penelope patted his arm. "It's cute that you believe that. Anyhow, if *you* put up fliers, you'll be worried about whether it's legal to put them places."

Jake was silent for two long seconds, then winced. "I mean, technically, there's an ordinance against posting bills on telephone poles..."

Laughing, Penelope took his hand. "See? We both know something being against the rules isn't going to bother me at all, and the faster the mulch gets off the driveway, the faster I'll forget to make jokes about it."

CHAPTER 17

*P*enelope carefully covered the anti-posting ordinance placard on the wooden telephone pole with her flier. The staple gun made a satisfying *thunk*. She tacked down four more spots. Rusted staples and chunks of missing wood showed past usage, but there wasn't anything else attached at the moment.

Esther waited in her wheelchair a few feet away. "If you use that many staples on all of them, you're going to run out."

Penelope patted her pocket. "It's okay. I brought the box of refills." She added another two staples on the bottom corners and they moved on. "That colored bark makes a nice contrast, but I wonder what it's going to look like after a few months."

"That colored bark is an abomination." Esther turned away from the house they were passing. "But I doubt any of the gardens in the competition are using it." She had her clipboard in her lap, the evaluation sheet for each house they had visited carefully filled out in her neat script.

Only some houses had blue flags near the curb, indicating they were part of the competition. All those houses had people stopped in front of them. Some viewers had driven, and others had ridden bicycles or were on foot. A group of twenty stood in a cluster further down the block, listening to a guide recite facts and figures about the house they were currently in front of.

But even the houses without blue flags showed evidence of recent yard work. Penelope wondered how many of the plants were actually supposed to be pruned at this time of year. They stopped in front of a Craftsman with a mossy stone wall, Japanese maples, a wishing well, paper lanterns, and — oddly — a statue of Ganesh surrounded by crimson poppies.

"It's very..." Penelope struggled to come up with the right word, aware that the house owners could very well be in the group of people gathered on the sidewalk. "Eclectic."

Esther snorted and kept writing.

From Penelope's point of view, the garden seemed fine, though the different elements clashed. The trees seemed healthy, but the red of the poppy flowers looked odd with the deep reddish purple of the maple. She wasn't a fan of the wishing well — it wasn't a well, really, just a little round structure with a hand crank on the side and a wooden bucket that wouldn't hold water even if there had been a well to dip it into — but she'd give them points for originality with the Ganesh statue. And at least they hadn't added the abomination of colored bark anywhere.

Penelope glanced at the heading on the page where Esther was still scribbling notes. The house belonged to Dot McGrath. After a moment, she placed the name. Penelope's son, Seth, had been on a soccer team coached by Dot's husband. Or possibly ex-husband now. She had vague memories of hearing something that had happened between the couple on a trip a few years after Seth had left the team. Even the most salacious stories faded over time.

Esther finished writing and moved her wheelchair forward at top speed. Penelope waited until they were clear of the group. "What's the verdict?"

"If you come back and look at it in two weeks, you'll either find dead moss or dead trees. There's no way to water that area without killing one of them."

Penelope glanced back over her shoulder. "But everything looks so healthy."

"Because they just put everything in three weeks ago. That wishing well is only there because one of the maples died immediately when it was transplanted. And the elephant statue is hiding the stump of another."

"It's probably good I'm not judging this contest."

Esther reached out to pat her arm. "Don't worry. There's no danger of that ever happening."

A couple walked by with a German Shepherd on a leash. Penelope didn't recognize the dog or the owners, but they nodded to Esther as they passed, and she saw a clipboard with judging sheets in the woman's hand.

"Is it weird that everyone who is missing a dog is a possible judge?" Then Penelope remembered Josie. "Ugh. Never mind. Josie has only been here three years." She and Esther had already discussed the furry costumes and looked over some examples on the internet before they'd left the house.

Esther held up a hand. "Don't discount her that quickly. If she belonged to a gardening society wherever she lived before this, that might count. And she has just the kind of talent we hope to attract to our club. She could very well be a judge."

Penelope thought about how Josie had been when they'd left her that morning. "If she was signed up for it, I think having Piggins disappear might have derailed her plans. But even so." Was the link between them all as simple as being on the secret judges panel? "I know you're not allowed to say who is and isn't a judge, but... Everyone assumes Isolde is on the panel. Then there's Jillian and Bill. And Josie. How about Connie Tile and Laurence Skelton and Carol Entweiler?"

Esther guided her wheelchair up an empty driveway and turned around so she would see if anyone got close. "If you tell anyone this information, I'll get kicked out of the rose garden society and I'll spend the rest of my days making you miserable."

Penelope leaned closer. "I'll never say a word. Other than to Jake, of course."

"Of course." Esther waited for two people to ride by on a tandem bicycle. "Now, you know I don't know exactly who is a judge and who is an alternate, but we *have* had a few meetings with everyone there, and both Connie and Laurence were there. Plus Josie, Bill, and Jillian."

Penelope nodded slowly. "And Isolde, I'm assuming."

Esther pursed her lips and shook her head. "She took herself off the panel this year. She's been planning to cut back on her involvement for a while, but a couple of months ago she thought she was going to need surgery, so she didn't bother to turn in an application."

Penelope raised her eyebrows. "Interesting." She went through the rest of the list in her head. "And Carol?"

"Wasn't at the meetings. She was an alternate last year, and the year before, if I remember correctly, but she decided not to this year."

So all the dogs that had disappeared on Wednesday night belonged to people who might be judging the competition. But the two dogs that had disappeared on Friday morning were owned by people who weren't. That *had* to be significant.

They headed to the next house on Esther's list, Penelope stopping to attach a flier to each telephone pole.

By the time Esther had written her opinion about the last house on her list, stating that the lingering smell of pesticides ruined any beauty present in the roses crowded together in a line — Esther, while not toeing the only organic line, had strong opinions on the overuse of pesticides — Penelope had run out of fliers.

She needed to talk to Jake about the likelihood of the judges being targeted on Wednesday night. Penelope still didn't see a motive, but it was too strange to be a coincidence.

And then they would need to see if the lost dog fliers bore fruit.

CHAPTER 18

$\mathcal{M}$ulch mountain had disappeared from the driveway by the time Penelope made it home, and a freshly showered Jake was staring into the refrigerator. Brutus stood next to him. "We might be having peanut butter and jelly sandwiches for dinner."

Penelope shrugged. Grocery shopping had taken a back seat to all the other chores for the past week. "There are worse things to eat."

They both looked at Brutus.

Jake's phone rang. He closed the refrigerator door and answered it. "Really, where?" He paused. "And does the dog have three white feet? Hm… I don't think that's Diogy, but I'll drive over that way and see. Thanks for calling." He put his phone down on the counter.

Penelope sighed. "Not the person trying to get money."

"No. The flaw in our plan is there's a tan Chihuahua running around by the school right now. That's the third person who's called. We may have to go catch that dog and find out who it belongs to just so people stop calling me." He rubbed at his forehead with one palm. "How did I become the guy who tracks down stray dogs and cats?"

Penelope hugged him. "It's because you're a good person."

He leaned back against the counter and laughed, but put his arms around her. "The eau de stale beer perfume you're wearing is really something."

Penelope wrinkled her nose. "I was hoping it would wear off while I was out walking. I can't smell it anymore."

"Definitely still there."

"I'll go take a shower while you sort out the peanut butter and jelly situation." She straightened, but Jake didn't drop his arms.

"Or… I could help you in the shower and then we could order pizza." Jake's eyebrows rose while he watched her face.

"Mmm." Penelope tapped her lip, considering. "What toppings are you thinking of on this pizza?"

Jake broadened his stance to bring his face closer to hers. "Anything you want."

"Oh, well then. You know I'm never going to turn down pizza." Penelope grinned and leaned toward him. "And it might take two people to get all this dried beer off me."

Jake's phone rang. Penelope laughed as he groaned and picked up the phone.

"Hello?… It's definitely not the one running around by the school… Oh?" Jake stood up straight. He hit the speaker button on his phone and put it down on the counter. "Can you repeat that?"

"I said, I think I found your dog. Three white feet and a pink collar. That's yours, right?" The male voice sounded young, though Penelope had accepted most people sounded young to her these days. In the background, she could hear someone talking, and a rhythmic mechanical noise.

Jake muted the line. "Can I borrow your phone?" Then he

unmuted. "That sounds like Diogy. Is he okay? When can I come get him?"

Penelope handed him her phone without thinking. Those background noises sounded familiar, like it was some place she knew.

"I'm going to need you to go get me some gift cards first. Then I'll bring Diogy to you."

"But… but…"

"If you don't get the gift cards, you'll never see your dog again."

Jake dialed the number displayed on his phone, then showed her the *call cannot be completed* message. He hit mute again. "I think he's using a computer, not a cellphone. I doubt this is traceable."

"I know that place," Penelope muttered.

Jake unmuted the call. "Okay, okay! I'll have to go to the store to buy them… Can I call you back when I have them? What's the best number?"

The sound of a squeaking wheel came through the line as the stranger talked. "Just stay on the line while you go to the store. If the checker asks, tell her you're buying gift cards for your relatives."

"Okay. I just need to get my shoes on first." Jake hit the mute button. "This sounds like the same person who called Bill. I think we can safely assume the gift cards are unrelated to the missing dogs."

The squeaking wheel came through the line again and finally shook something loose in Penelope's brain. "He's at the library, at the computers in the back next to the copy machine."

Jake looked at her. "You amaze me. Road trip?" He unmuted the call. "Okay, I'm leaving now."

CHAPTER 19

Two hours later, they were back at the house, Jake carrying a bottle of wine, and Penelope carrying Thai food. Jake's phone rang again as they came into the house. "Hello? No, no, we already got Diogy back. Thanks for checking." He hung up and put the bottle down on the table next to the food. "I need to disconnect that number before I do anything else."

Penelope sniffed her forearm. "Guard the food. I'll be back in two minutes." She ran upstairs, rinsed off in the shower, and came back down in a robe.

Jake had split the food onto two plates and stored the leftovers in the refrigerator. Brutus was lying next to his empty bowl, watching Jake. "Don't be fooled," Jake said. "I just fed him."

"That poor starving dog." Penelope picked up her plate and inhaled the scent of Thai basil and eggplant. "I think that kid was more scared of his mother than being arrested."

After confronting the teen, who had still been on the phone with Jake when they found him, Jake and Penelope had debated what to do with him. Penelope had argued for bringing his family into the discussion. Jake had pointed out while they only knew of two cases, there were undoubtedly more, and the police should be involved. The kid had begged them to just let him go and promised to pay everyone back.

In the end, they'd called his mother. She had shown up and said they were going straight to the police station.

Jake poured wine into two glasses. "A fourteen-year-old with no priors is going to get sent through the community diversion program. My mom would have had me doing chores every weekend for years to pay everyone back."

They moved out to the living room and took their usual places, with Jake sitting forward in the corner and Penelope leaning on his shoulder with her feet on the next cushion. Brutus curled up on the end of the couch, gazing longingly at her plate. "My mom would have just looked disappointed and I would have immediately regretted everything." Penelope took a sip of wine. "It took me *years* to perfect that look with Seth."

Jake turned on a golf game and sighed. "So far, we've managed to figure out everything that *isn't* connected to the case. If we could make any sort of progress on actually *finding* the dogs, I'd be ecstatic."

"I do have one bit of information, though I don't really understand how it gets us anywhere." Between bites, Penelope told him about the first batch of dogs all belonging to people who might be judges, and the second batch belonging to non-judges.

On the screen, a golfer sank a ten-foot putt to the quiet approbation of the crowd.

"I agree, that can't be a coincidence." Jake was quiet again as he watched the camera pan over the golf course, following the flight of an errant drive. "But I don't know what to make of it." He blew out a frustrated breath. "Nothing in this case makes any sense."

"Why only take little dogs? Why steal them on two days? Why target people in the rose garden society?"

Jake echoed one of her questions. "Why steal them on two days?" He handed his plate to her and dug his notebook and pen out of his pocket. "We know this had nothing to do with the gift card extortion. And nothing to do with the cat." He crossed out sections on two pages. "So where does that leave us?"

Penelope turned so she could watch him write. "If we forget about the dogs taken on Friday, it all looks like an attempt to affect the judging of the festival contest. But the two dogs taken Friday morning ruin that theory."

"Or do they?" Jake flipped to a new page and drew a line to split it in two. In the upper section, he wrote *Wednesday - judges* and in the lower section he wrote *Friday - not judges*. He added the list of owners and dogs in the appropriate section. "Assume for the moment there are two things going on. Completely separate. So the motive up here is tampering with the contest results."

"But why?" Penelope stopped. "Never mind. I know there are people who might kill to win, so I suppose kidnapping a few dogs wouldn't be a stretch."

"Right. That just leaves us with Guinevere and Bella disappearing on Friday morning. Isolde and Carol *aren't* judges this year, so they wouldn't be able to change the contest results."

"Unless someone didn't…" Penelope stopped and groaned. "No. Whoever took the dogs on Wednesday knew a lot more about the judges than I did. If they knew Josie was in the group, they would have known Isolde and Carol weren't."

Jake leaned forward to pick up the wine bottle and poured some into her glass. "You're still trying to connect them." He put the bottle down and folded the page in his notebook so only the Friday information was visible. "If it was just these two, what would you think?"

Penelope laughed. "I'd assume Carol's mother had finally taken out a hit on Bella, and Isolde's grandkids got tired of her paying attention to the dog instead of them."

Jake turned his head to look at her for a moment, then turned back and circled *Isolde (Guinevere)* on the Friday section. He unfolded the page. "Let me tell you a hypothetical story and you tell me if it makes sense."

"Go ahead."

"I'm Tamsin or Leo, or possibly Tamsin *and* Leo. I start businesses that interest me. They aren't successful, but that's okay, because they don't need to be. My grandmother will give me more money if I need it."

Penelope finished the last of the noodles and put her plate on the floor. She just barely kept her wine from spilling when Brutus jumped off the cushion so he could lick the plate. "So far, so good."

"Except lately my grandmother is a little reluctant to pay my bills. My latest business is stalling because I can't afford the permits and rent and everything else."

Penelope nodded. "And your grandmother is enamored with her new dog."

"Yes. In fact, my grandmother loves her new dog so much, she would rather spend her days with the dog than me."

"Because you're a jerk who only wants her money. And maybe she noticed that."

"True, but I'm not introspective enough to see that. So. The garden festival is coming up. And a bunch of dogs disappear. Everyone is talking about them. And I get to thinking that it's a shame that my grandmother's dog wasn't one of them." He handed his plate to Penelope, and she put it down for Brutus to pre-clean.

"So you decide to take her dog because you're a horrible person."

"Yes. And I decide to steal a *second* dog because otherwise people might not link my grandmother's dog disappearing with the others."

"Except you don't realize that Carol isn't a judge, so you take Bella and confuse us all."

"Exactly." He stopped. "Does that hold together?"

Penelope thought about it as she drank her wine. "I would believe that story, sure. But we don't have a shred of evidence."

Jake converted the circle around Isolde's name into a flower. "No. But that seems like something we might be able to check. What would Tamsin and Leo do with the dogs?"

Penelope held her glass out for a refill. "I'm going on the assumption that the dogs are alive and well, just hidden." She wasn't even going to allow for any other possibility. "Tamsin and Leo probably wouldn't keep the dogs at home, just in case. And Bella, at least, would bark her head off if left alone, so I doubt they could keep them in the commercial property downtown, even if they have the keys."

"They aren't at *this* shelter, but maybe a different one?"

Penelope shook her head. "I know Bella has a microchip. A shelter would scan for it first thing. Maybe have a friend keep them?"

"Possibly." He scribbled an illegible note at the bottom of the page. "They'd have to be a pretty good friend, though. Someone who wouldn't back out if the police got involved."

Penelope laughed. "They'd have to be a *really* good friend to deal with Bella. Bella might require money to change hands." She sat up. "That's it! If I were them, I would board the dogs, at least in the short term."

Jake wrote another note. "Someplace far enough away that people wouldn't be talking about the missing dogs."

"But not *too* far away." Penelope settled back against Jake's shoulder. "Remember, Tamsin and Leo were driving around half the night to buy those toys for the booths on Thursday and then they had to be up in time to take both dogs before eight the next morning. They probably didn't get much sleep. I doubt they drove more than an hour to get to a boarding facility." She thought about it a little more. "That still leaves a whole lot of places to check."

"But it's a finite list. At least it's something."

"We could be completely wrong about this."

Jake nodded. "We could."

"But it makes sense. That leaves us with the Wednesday night group. If we're right about the motive being affecting the judging…"

Jake nodded again. "If we're right, then our judges are going to hear from the dognapper before they turn in their evaluation forms tomorrow afternoon. Maybe they already have, and they were too scared to tell us."

"We'll have to ask them." Penelope looked at the time. "In the morning," she amended. "And we can call the boarding facilities in the morning, too. If we're wrong about that, nobody ever has to know." She paused. "In the meantime…"

"Mm?" Jake's attention was on the golfer lining up his shot.

"I have an idea for something we can do tonight."

"What's that?" Jake's eyes briefly flicked to her, then returned as she gained his entire attention. Without looking, he hit the button on the remote to turn off the television. "I'll take care of the dishes if you settle the dog."

Brutus jumped off the couch and ran to the freezer. Penelope laughed.

CHAPTER 20

Early the next morning, Penelope had just finished printing out the list of boarding facilities within seventy-five miles when Esther called. "I need some help outside. As soon as possible."

When Penelope and Jake arrived, the first light of dawn illuminated the destruction of Esther's garden. Plants had been trampled, holes dug, and mulch scattered everywhere. If it hadn't been for the paw prints, Penelope would have assumed a herd of wild boars had come through town.

Esther sat in her wheelchair between Jake and Penelope, glumly cataloging the damage. "I think the red lobelia is done for, but maybe the blue will recover if we replant it."

Penelope nodded, as if she had some idea of which plants Esther was talking about. Jake knew, and it was really Jake who Esther had needed to come over and help fix the damage. Penelope knew she was there more for moral support, and also because Esther would never dream of a pre-dawn call to Jake.

Jake could deal with the plants, but Penelope was more interested in what had happened. Muddy paw prints on the sidewalk suggested at least two dogs had been involved. "Why would dogs suddenly decide to dig up your garden on the weekend of the festival competition?"

There was no shortage of loose dogs on any given night, thanks to the crimes against fence-building of Red and Sons, but this was the first time she'd seen a dog tear up a garden like this. And the digging had been localized to just Esther's garden — the houses Jake and Penelope had passed on the way to Esther's had been untouched, even though many of them had the same types of plants.

Esther shook her head. "Bad luck, I suppose." She was still concentrating on how to fix things. "The alyssum is a total loss, I imagine, but maybe we can replant something from the backyard to fill in the holes. What a mess."

Jake made his way through the wreckage. "How about I get the blue lobelia back in the ground, bring a couple of your smaller red dahlias up here to replace those..."

Penelope tuned the other two out as she picked her way through the yard. The damage hadn't been random. Some plants had been dug up almost completely, but others hadn't been touched. She leaned down to look at the biggest hole and then put her nose closer and sniffed. An earthy aroma filled her nostrils with a sinus-clearing addition that reminded her of a poorly cleaned fish cleaning station. "Why do I smell fish?"

Esther paused in the middle of her ideas to reorder the plants. "Fish?"

"Yes. It's not that strong, but I can smell it."

Jake crouched down on the other side of the yard. "I can smell it over here, too." He stood up. "Did you use a fish-based fertilizer?"

Esther shook her head. "I haven't used any fertilizer on it in the last few weeks. No point in taking the risk of the plants burning at the last minute."

Penelope moved to a different spot and sniffed. Same thing. "Unless your plants have suddenly decided to smell like fish, somebody has done something."

Esther looked at the yard. "I had Rebecca Tinsdale bring over a bit of new mulch a few days ago, and then Rufus came over to spread it around. Could that be it? I didn't notice it particularly smelling of fish, but I was inside for most of the time." She folded her hands in her lap. "Rufus is not always a very pleasant person to be around, so I'm afraid I pretended I had work to do and left him to get on with things out here."

Rufus hadn't said two words to Penelope the entire time he and his mother had been delivering the mulch at Jake and Penelope's house. Penelope would have made an excuse and left, too. "Maybe there was something mixed in with it."

Esther pointed at a hole dug next to the sidewalk. "I *thought* I'd seen more stray cats in the yard for the last few days." She turned her wheelchair in a circle. "I hope the smell goes away soon, but at least this is the last day of the festival judging." She looked back at Jake. "I think you might be able to dig up the small camellia in the back and bring that over there."

Penelope went to get the shovel and broom out of the garage. She might not be able to keep a plant alive, but at least she could clean up all the dirt and mulch scattered on the sidewalk and paths.

CHAPTER 21

o thank Jake and Penelope for their help in the garden, Esther took the third sheet of boarding facilities and started making calls, while Jake sat at the kitchen table across from her to work on his page. Penelope got too distracted by them talking, so she went into the living room and let the cats drape themselves over her shoulders and legs as she went through her own list.

By Penelope's fifth call, she had her introduction down. "Hi, this is Penelope Standing, and I'm looking for some dogs that were stolen from this area on Friday morning that we think might be boarding with you. One is a Pomeranian and the other is a shih tzu." She paused to take a breath, and to let the person on the end of the line catch up. From the other calls, she suspected the person answering the kennel phone on Sunday morning would be young and fairly uncomfortable talking on the phone. Only one person she had spoken to had suggested that privacy concerns would keep her from answering either way. The rest had freely admitted they didn't have any such boarders.

This kennel had the now-familiar chorus of dogs barking

and howling in the background. The young woman spoke loudly to be heard over them. "You said a Pomeranian and a shih tzu?"

"Yes." Encouraged by the question, Penelope continued. "The shih tzu has probably never touched the ground before, but the Pomeranian would be trying to kill anyone who comes near her."

"Oh. I don't think so. We have a Pomeranian here, but she's the sweetest little dog and her owners are long-time clients."

Penelope sighed. "Doesn't sound like the same dog. Thanks for checking."

"You're welcome. Good luck."

Penelope disconnected. She drew a line through that kennel and started dialing the next one.

In the kitchen, she could hear Jake taking a break from the boarding kennel list to talk to each of the people whose dogs went missing on Wednesday night. It didn't sound as if any of them had been contacted by the dognapper. Jake asked them to text him if that changed. Today was the final day of judging. If the disappearance of the dogs wasn't related to the festival, Jake and Penelope were back to square one.

On Penelope's phone, another young woman answered, and another chorus of dogs nearly drowned out her voice. "Happy Acres Dog Boarding, how can I help you today?"

"Hi, this is Penelope Standing, and I'm looking for some dogs that were stolen from this area on Friday morning. We think they might be boarding with you — a Pomeranian and a shih tzu."

"Not here. We just have hunting dogs, and I can't see either of those as hunting breeds."

Bella would probably take on a bear, but nobody would ever mistake her for a hunting dog. "Thanks for your time." She disconnected. Penelope crossed the name off the list.

In the kitchen, Esther settled her phone back in the cradle. "Found them!"

Penelope slid out from under the pile of cats and went back to the kitchen.

Esther circled the kennel and passed the sheet across the table to Jake. "A woman brought them in Friday morning. The staff already thought something might be fishy because they tried to put them in the same cage and the dogs immediately started fighting with each other."

Penelope looked at Jake. "Now what? Do we call Isolde and Carol and tell them we found their dogs, or go make sure they're really there first?"

Jake stood up. "I think the best thing would be if I went to the kennel and talked to them. I don't know if they'll let me bring the dogs back, but maybe I can at least get photos and we can get confirmation." He cleared his throat, as if he were trying to find the best way to phrase something. "I'll probably have to get the police here and maybe the local police there involved, and we all know you…"

Esther snorted.

Penelope smiled. "Yes, we do all know how that would go." As former law enforcement, Jake knew who to talk to and how to get things done. Penelope tended to see law enforcement obstacles as brick walls to repeatedly throw herself at until the wall got out of her way. "Fine. We'll go the sensible route and have you go. Esther and I have a few more gardens to look at anyhow." Penelope also had a few dogs and cats to check in on, but her schedule was loose. Not many people left town during the festival weekend.

Jake patted the pockets where he kept his wallet and keys, then picked up his phone. "I'll call when I get there. Let me know if anything changes here."

* * *

After Jake had left, Penelope and Esther headed out in the opposite direction of the route they had taken the day before. The repairs to Esther's garden hadn't taken all that long; it was still early enough that the streets were empty of everyone except a few people headed to church services. With the award presentation scheduled for late afternoon, most of the people interested in gardens elected to finish their tours in the afternoon and end at the beer tent just in time to find out the results at the ceremony.

"It will be nicer not having to deal with the crowds," Esther said as they sped along in the street. At the wheelchair's top speed, Penelope had to jog to keep up. "If I heard another person talk about how nice the daisies looked, I was going to start correcting them."

Penelope winced. "What's wrong with daisies? I *like* daisies."

Esther glanced over with a smile. "There's absolutely nothing wrong with daisies, but nothing we looked at yesterday was a daisy."

Penelope mentally crossed daisies off the list of plants she could name and kept jogging. "Do we have any contenders for the top garden on our list today?"

"Two. Melvyn Reinhardt grows a beautiful organic fruit and flower display, and Ada Sniatecki has that lovely wisteria tunnel. There are a few others I need to judge, but they should be quick."

Melvyn's fruit and flower display was indeed impressive. Flowers that a less discerning person might have called daisies carpeted the ground under miniature apple, persimmon, and orange trees, but the main attraction was a rosebush that had roses so dark they were almost black.

"I didn't even know black roses were a thing." Penelope crept across the yard to look more closely, leaving Esther on the sidewalk pretending not to know her. "Do you think I can get Jake to plant something like this?" Close up, the roses were a dark red instead of black, but they really *were* beautiful. Penelope used one finger on the wet stem to move the rose closer so she could smell it.

"You! Get back on the sidewalk!"

Penelope jumped. Straightening, she saw a bald man in a tattered bathrobe standing near the door. He waved his hand imperiously at her, as if a force field extending from his body would push her off his yard. While he lacked hair on his head, the same wasn't true of the rest of his body. With every movement, the robe opened a little farther. "Sorry!" Penelope trotted back to the safety of the street before the robe finished its structural failure.

The door slammed shut.

Esther finished making notes on her clipboard. "I really can't take you anywhere, can I?"

"I wasn't hurting his precious plant." Penelope pushed a strand of hair behind her ear, then stopped and smelled her hand. "When someone says everything is organic, do you actually do tests?"

"With our budget? Of course not. Why?" Esther slowly lowered her clipboard. "Are you saying…?"

Penelope jogged across the yard, plucked a leaf from the rosebush, and gave it to Esther.

The door burst open and the man ran out again, still in his poorly secured robe and bare feet. "If you don't stay off my property, I'm calling the police!" He came to a halt when he saw Esther. "Ah, Esther. How lovely to see you. Are you here with this… woman?"

Esther took a long sniff of the leaf and dropped her hand. "Melvyn! What do you think you're doing?" Even talking to a middle-aged man, she retained the air of the kindergarten teacher she had been. "Do you think I don't recognize the smell of this insecticide? And it's the old formulation, isn't it? How long have you had that bottle around?"

The man ran forward. "Shh. Don't —" He came to a stop next to Esther's wheelchair and spoke in an urgent whisper. "Aphids, Esther. Aphids. From out of nowhere and just all over the plant. I had to do *something*."

Esther moved the chair back a few inches. "I sympathize, Melvyn, but you can't very well enter the contest in the organic category and then spray carbaryl all over one of your plants."

Melvyn advanced, his voice still barely above a whisper. "Isn't there some way you could just forget about this? I know you've always wanted cuttings from my —"

Esther cut him off. "Melvyn! I *know* you wouldn't stoop to trying to bribe a rose festival judge." She stared at him.

Penelope looked from one to the other. "Could he switch to a different category?"

Melvyn's hands came up over his face. "I'm ruined." The movement opened his robe a little more.

Esther cleared her throat. "If you withdraw from the competition, I don't think I would have any reason to discuss your entry with the other judges."

Melvyn lifted his head and looked at Penelope. She mimed zipping her lips closed, locking them, and throwing away the key. Not that she would have bothered to talk about the non-organic status of someone's yard in any case, but the sooner this was resolved, the more likely she and Esther were to get away before Melvyn's robe parted completely.

"Thank you! Thank you!"

Esther drew a line through the sheet on her clipboard and turned her chair. "Come along, Penelope."

Penelope managed to keep a straight face until they were two houses away. "I have never been so anxious to finish a conversation in my life."

Esther laughed. "We were about to find out whether the wedding vegetables were organic as well." She snorted and looked at her clipboard. "Come on. Maybe we can get through the rest of these before the early morning church services let out and traffic picks up again."

CHAPTER 22

The rest of the judging was uneventful, at least as far as Penelope was concerned. Esther tsked over the state of one person's aphid-covered roses and sighed over the presence of bright orange bark covering a small area at another house. Penelope carefully didn't say anything about daisies. She found some of the gardens beautiful, and others not as interesting. After a while, it was like looking at too many paintings in a museum — everything blurred together.

Jake pulled up just as Penelope and Esther were getting back to Esther's house. They waited as he got out and locked the car. "It's definitely Bella and Guinevere. I confirmed the microchip numbers. It's a different county, so their animal control is taking possession of the dogs and bringing them back here later today." He smiled. "And I don't have to do any of the paperwork. Though I *do* owe a few people beer or coffee."

They went inside the house and headed to the kitchen, where Esther poured three glasses of lemonade. "And were you able to identify the woman who brought them in?"

Jake made the face that Penelope called his "I'm trying to

be fair to all parties" expression. "From the description, it could have been Tamsin. But it could have been a lot of other women as well. They have a camera in the lobby, but only one person knows how to access the recording and she's away for the weekend." He held up his hands, palm outward. "Isolde just asked me to find the dogs. She never said anything about catching the person responsible."

Penelope struggled to keep a straight face at that. The first thing Isolde would do after she had Guinevere back would be to ask who had taken her. Rightly so, in Penelope's opinion. Even if there wasn't enough evidence to bring charges, Isolde needed to know if she could trust her grand-children. "You told Carol and Isolde you found the dogs?"

"I did. I even sent pictures to make sure we hadn't somehow found a different set of mismatched dogs. Bella tried to eat my hand when I put my phone into her kennel to get a picture without the bars in the way. That was when I knew for sure. Unless Bella has an evil twin somewhere."

"I'm pretty sure Bella *is* the evil twin," Penelope said. "You didn't see any of the other missing dogs while you were back there?" Their assumption that the dogs were taken by different people was just that — an assumption.

Jake shook his head. "No. And I looked. I think we were right about the other dogs being part of the contest." He looked around. "Did I miss anything while I was gone? Nobody got in touch saying they'd had a ransom demand, did they?"

"No. Just the great non-organic insecticide scandal, and I don't think that has anything to do with the dogs." Penelope told him about Melvyn's black roses. "The flowers are really nice, but if we would have to keep dumping chemicals on the rosebush to keep it alive, I don't think I want one after all."

Esther hummed in agreement. "That's the problem with all the novelty colors. Even if they're grafted on hardy rootstock, they still aren't as strong as a plant bred to withstand the local environment." She shook her head. "It's such a shame that Melvyn stooped to such practices. He was one of the frontrunners going into the competition."

Jake's phone vibrated. He tapped on it, then pushed it across the table so Esther and Penelope could read it. The text from Jillian read: *Just found this note on the windshield.* The accompanying picture showed a page with computer-printed text. *If you want to see your dog again, make sure the winner doesn't have grapevines. Don't tell the police.*

Penelope looked at the picture in disbelief. "You know how I said I had no idea what was going on before? Well, now we have more information and I understand it even less."

Jake drew his phone back. "I have to admit, I assumed the demands would be to make one specific person win. But this... Does someone hate wine that badly?"

Penelope looked at Esther. "Do any of the frontrunners have grapes?"

Esther raised an eyebrow. "We were at the Connor house yesterday, remember? They have the awning with the grapes, and the metal sculpture you said looked like gigantic silverware."

"Oh, right." Penelope raised her chin. "The house with all the colorful flowers that the uneducated people near us thought were daisies." That was the part she really remembered.

Jake's cough sounded suspiciously like laughter.

"Exactly." Esther looked at the table for a moment. "I think there's only one other house in the top twenty that has grapes in the front yard, and there was no way all the judges were ever going to agree on that one." She looked up at Jake. "It has gnome statues, and some people have very strong feelings about those."

Penelope tried not to get sidetracked by the garden gnomes, though she was tempted to find out who didn't like them. "If nobody was interfering with the judges, would the Connors win?"

Esther pursed her lips. "Maybe, but it's not a sure thing." She sighed. "It really depends on who the actual judges are, you know. We don't all score everything the same way."

Jake took out his notebook. "How about we come at this in a different way. Can you make a list of the top ten, roughly in the order you expect them to come out in this contest? Not necessarily *your* top ten, but the ones everyone is most likely to agree on."

While Esther was working on that, Jake's phone buzzed again. This time the text was from Josie, and the note said *If you want to see your dog again, make sure the winner doesn't have a bridge. Don't tell the police.*

Penelope and Jake stared at it. The only sound was Esther's pen scratching as she wrote her list.

Penelope shook her head. "It has to be the same person — the wording is too similar to be more than one person doing this. But I don't understand why they didn't just tell Josie who they want to win."

Jake picked up Esther's clipboard and looked at the scoring sheet. "This is why. Ten categories are given a score between zero and nine. Add them all up, and you get a final score from each judge between zero and ninety-nine."

Penelope eyed him. "I got my son through algebra with a passing grade. I had figured out the scoring."

"But look at them." Jake flipped through the stack. "The frontrunners have almost all eights and nines. The final numbers are almost certainly clustered together in the nineties."

"Yes."

"So it would be nearly impossible for one judge's scores to

be high enough to make a particular person win. There just isn't enough room between the current values and a perfect score. You'd have to convince all the judges to work together if you wanted to fix the contest that way."

Penelope sat back in her chair. "Not all the judges have dogs."

"Exactly. But while one judge can't make one score rise to the top..."

Penelope suddenly saw where he was going with this. "One judge could tank a competitor and knock them out of the running."

Jake nodded. "And it makes it a lot harder to point the finger at the person behind this."

Penelope thought about it for a moment longer. "But... Someone is going through all this just to make sure a few people lose? Why? That still doesn't ensure any particular person wins."

Jake took a deep breath as if he were about to explain something, then let it out. "That's the part I haven't figured out yet. I'm pretty sure there must be a reason, though. I'm hoping it will be more obvious when we look at Esther's list."

While they waited for Esther to finish coming up with her best guess for the top ten, Jake called the other two judges whose dogs were missing and had them check for notes. Both found one. Connie's said she couldn't allow anyone with a tree swing to win. Laurence's note indicated a fountain should be avoided.

When Esther had finished, she crossed out the ones that would be knocked out of the competition if the dognapper got their way. Then the three of them stared at the results.

Esther had placed her own garden at a modest ninth place. Penelope looked at a name that had been printed at the halfway mark and scribbled out. "Who else were you going to put there?"

"Aabira. But then I remembered all the damage to her lavender bushes. Probably from the same dogs that dug up my yard last night. She doesn't have a bridge, grapevines, tree swing, or fountain. She would be near the top if her garden hadn't been destroyed."

They stared at the list.

Esther finally shook her head. "I just don't see how this is supposed to work. It doesn't knock out the top four and leave a clear frontrunner among the rest. This might change the winner, yes, but the ones remaining are so close that I still can't say for sure who will win the final prize."

They stared at the list again. The grey tabby jumped onto the table, sat down on the still-folded newspaper, and began to wash himself.

"Maybe someone who bet too much on the results?" Penelope could hear the doubt in her voice, even as she spoke. "Though most of the bets I've heard of are for just a few dollars. I've never heard of anything above ten."

"You'd lose almost that much on dog food," Jake pointed out. He moved his chair back so the calico could jump in his lap more easily.

Esther shook her head. "The only real difference I can see is these changes would mean Anna Durich wouldn't end up as Gardener of the Year. The committee won't have to deal with her speeches about space aliens while they're trying to make decisions about the parks."

Penelope grinned. Anna didn't have pets, so Penelope had never dealt with her in a professional capacity. She'd talked to her more than a few times at the farmers' market, though, and been thoroughly entertained. Anna's beliefs were a mixture of every book she'd read, and were rife with contradictions, but she was excited about everything. "I like Anna."

Esther raised one eyebrow. "Everyone likes Anna until

they have to get something done with her input. When her kids were in school, she was asked not to volunteer again."

"What? That was *possible*?" Penelope's outrage was only partially feigned. She'd spent years volunteering in classrooms, trying to help children do things she wasn't particularly good at doing herself.

Esther's sigh turned into a laugh. "I think the final straw was when she was supposed to be helping the first graders make handprint turkeys for Thanksgiving. Instead, they all made pyramid hats because she'd been reading some book about pyramid power."

Penelope giggled. "That must have gone over really well with the parents."

A crease formed in Jake's brow. "Pyramid power?"

Penelope waved a hand in dismissal. "Don't even try to understand it. Anna once told me the vibration of my aura was very calming, and one of my parents had probably been dark fey. You just have to roll with it."

Jake lifted the hand that wasn't petting the calico. "Oh, I've had more than a few conversations with her. She tried to get me to switch the police department to using 'peace phasers' every time I went to community events. I just never heard about the pyramid thing."

Esther frowned. "It didn't last long. In any case, her brain may be a little loose, but she would be a serious contender for gardener of the year without these changes." She shook her head. "Maybe this is a good thing. The committee is already pretty divided about where the new recreation center is supposed to be. I can't even imagine trying to make decisions with Anna there, making sure ley lines and feng shui and alien landing sites were all taken into account."

Jake leaned back in his chair and let the calico settle against his chest. "Oh, right. The winner ends up on the committee for the year, don't they? I'd forgotten about that.

The committee is in charge of some large budgets. Maybe this is about money, after all."

"Technically, they just advise the city council," Penelope said.

Jake raised one eyebrow. "But..." He winced as the calico started kneading his chest, though he didn't move the cat away.

Penelope nodded. "But the council would need to have a really good reason not to follow their advice. The rose garden society fundraising accounts for a significant portion of the parks department operating budget. They wouldn't want to mess with that."

Jake looked at Esther. "Other than the new recreation center, are there any decisions coming up that will depend on the Gardener of the Year casting the deciding vote?"

Esther shook her head. "Almost everything else is just deciding whether to renew existing contracts, and I don't think any of those are controversial. The Gardener of the Year also has to do a bunch of ceremonial appearances, but mostly they just get told where to stand and who to smile at. The recreation center is the only thing on the docket that people are going to argue about."

Jake nodded. "I think we need to know more about the recreation center."

CHAPTER 23

As an active member of the rose garden society, Esther had access to the meeting notes and agendas, as well as the rules for making decisions. "Everything about the process is supposed to be transparent," she said as she brought out the manilla envelope stuffed with notes for the year. "So there's a process they go through to build up a matrix that factors in the cost of the land, insurance, parking, and everything else that could affect the decision."

Having dealt with more than a few failed attempts to force decision making to be fair and transparent, Penelope was skeptical. "Does it work?"

Esther drew in a breath. "I think it just wears everyone out until the people who care the most get their way, but it probably does cut down on the worst shenanigans."

Jake tipped the contents of the envelope onto the table. The grey tabby thrust out one paw and pulled a piece of paper toward him. Penelope picked him up, found a ball with a bell, and sent him off to play in the living room. The cat ignored the ball and jumped back on the table. Penelope repeated the process with a feather toy, and this time it worked.

Jake found the site proposal document and flipped through it. "Looks like there are three main sites that qualified. One close to downtown, one to the north, and the other on the east edge of town." He glanced at Esther for confirmation.

She nodded. "The central site would cost more for the land and be easier for people to get to. The north site would be slightly cheaper to build, but it would be convenient for the people in that area and nobody else. The east site would provide the most land for the money, so it would have an Olympic-size pool, but it would cause a transportation issue. Those are the main points."

Penelope knew how this sort of thing worked. "Except there are also a bunch of little things, aren't there?"

Esther nodded. "Some people want it as far away from downtown as possible because they're worried about encouraging teenagers to congregate near their businesses. Other people don't want to have another attraction siphoning business away from downtown." She rolled her eyes. "Half the point of the recreation center is giving the teenagers something to do other than wander around and get in trouble. And it isn't as if the kids are going to use a center on the edge of town if it's too inconvenient to get there."

"And how are people on the committee leaning right now?"

"Three for the east site, two for the north, and three for downtown."

Penelope pulled the top ten list closer to her. "Do you know how all these people would vote?"

Esther leaned forward to look at what she had written. "Ed Varhol spoke in favor of the downtown site a few months ago. Anna Durich... Trying to apply logic to her decisions is difficult, but I suspect she would be in favor of the downtown location. Tom Stalowy has children who swim competitively. He's been pushing for the east site."

As Esther went down the list, Penelope marked each one as downtown, east, or north.

Penelope looked at the results. Then she squinted and looked at them from a different angle. "I don't see an obvious pattern in the ones who would be excluded."

Esther shook her head. "Neither do I."

The grey tabby jumped back on the table and knocked a stack of papers onto the floor. Holding the cat in one hand, Penelope picked up the papers and handed them to Jake to put back in the envelope. "I'm going to go walk some dogs and hope that something occurs to me."

They had five hours before the Gardener of the Year was crowned.

CHAPTER 24

More people crowded the sidewalks as the day wore on. After spending the first block of her three-mile run with Heidi jumping on and off the sidewalk to avoid people, Penelope guided the German Shepherd in a different direction. They could cut through the middle school and then past the warehouses to the northeast. On weekdays, the business traffic made that a dangerous route, but it would be better on the weekend.

A three-mile round trip wouldn't get them to the north recreation center site, but she thought about it as she jogged. Just west of the warehouses, a developer had planted a strip of redwoods and built houses on the other side. A new recreation center nearby would boost the prices of those houses, but the city would need to change the existing bus routes if anyone without a car wanted to use the place.

They passed a blackened spot on the pavement in front of the tile warehouse. Heidi glanced up to see if Penelope would consider stopping so she could sniff the area, then kept trotting. Penelope smiled. "Maybe on the way back." Brutus would have just yanked her in that direction. Then again,

Brutus would have forgotten they were running together and knocked her down at least four times before they made it this far. Heidi was a much better jogging partner than Brutus.

The warehouses gave way to a street of older homes, these ones originally built for the workers back when there had been more factories in the area. Penelope checked the distance on her phone. They would need to turn around soon.

One benefit of delivering mail to different routes was knowing how all the streets connected. Penelope headed around the next corner, planning a loop that would get them back to Heidi's house at a little over the intended distance, while giving the dog a different set of places to see and smell. They passed another spot where something had burned. This time Penelope stopped and let Heidi sniff the area while she looked around.

This had to be where another one of the cars had burned. "Why would someone burn cars?" Heidi's ears flicked back, but the dog kept sniffing.

Penelope knew she wasn't perfect. Back when the former mayor had forced her out of her house so the developers could profit from a new strip mall, she'd had daydreams of doing some damage. But it had always been aimed at specific people. And all she had ever actually done was embarrass the mayor in public.

Destroying random things felt like it would need a different motivation. The police procedurals Jake loved to ridicule would imply someone in town had mental health issues. Penelope had known people with a variety of mental health challenges — they seemed no more or less likely to do crimes than anyone else. In her experience, greed was a far more likely cause for anything not done in the heat of the moment.

Heidi peed on the edge of the lawn, then looked up at Penelope as if wondering why they were still standing there. They moved forward again, Penelope keeping an eye on the uneven sidewalk and Heidi trotting across the carefully mowed lawns beside her.

Jake had made a comment about the arson affecting the serious crime stats in zone five. That was a holdover from his days in the police department. The town had originally been divided into six pie wedges radiating from the center. The boundaries had shifted over the years to accommodate changing population densities and new growth, so now the pie pieces looked more like someone had used a spoon to serve everyone instead of using a knife to make neat lines. Penelope had spent a lot of time staring at the map in Jake's old office while waiting for him to be ready to go to lunch, but she couldn't remember enough details to be sure.

She put one earpiece in and dialed without slowing down.

Jake answered on the third ring. "Tell me some good news. I'm running out of ideas."

"No news, just a question."

He paused, as if something she said had derailed his thoughts. "Are you running away from someone?"

Penelope smiled, checked the cross street for traffic, and jumped down from the curb. "Just running. Heidi says hello. I think she's getting used to running at your pace. I'm not going fast enough for her today."

"Don't let her fool you. The last time I ran with her, my legs still hadn't recovered from digging in the yard. We barely made it above a zombie shuffle. What's the question?"

A cat ran out from under a parked car as they jogged by. Heidi merely followed its progress with her head, not changing her distance from Penelope by a millimeter. "The north site. What zone would it be in? Esther made it sound like it would be mostly used by the people in Greenvale, but the site itself would be in zone five, wouldn't it?" Greenvale, where the houses were more expensive and the yards more uniformly coddled, took up most of zone four.

"Hang on. Let me look at the address." There was the sound of papers shuffling. "It would be... You're right. The site itself is in zone five. Huh."

Penelope's shoes slapped the pavement rhythmically while Jake was silent. "It's a long shot," she said.

"Tying in the arsons? I agree, but... It's the closest thing I've heard to a motive yet."

"But is it really? I'm not sure the details work out."

More paper shuffling. "I need to look at the selection criteria more closely. But let's assume, for the sake of argument, that crime in zone five raises insurance rates enough to knock the north site out of the process altogether. I'll talk to Esther about how that changes things. We may need to look at property records to find out who owns the other sites."

"And anything around there. Once the recreation center goes in, everything in the area should see more foot traffic." She guided Heidi onto the street to leave room on the sidewalk for a man with a stroller.

"That could be a challenge on Sunday." He paused. "I might know someone I can call."

Penelope hopped back up onto the sidewalk. "It may turn out to be a dead end."

"It's better than anything I've come up with. Maybe I should exercise more to jumpstart my brain."

Penelope grinned. "I know another kind of exercise we could do."

Jake's voice deepened. "Yeah?" Then he paused, and his voice went back to normal. "You're talking about planting a pomegranate tree, aren't you?"

Laughing, she said, "You'll just have to find out." Then she disconnected the call. "Come on, Heidi. Let's see how fast we can do the last block."

Heidi's ears went up and she lunged forward. Penelope grinned and sprinted to keep up.

fter a more sedate stroll around the block with a rotund dachshund, and a stop to give subcutaneous fluids to a cat, Penelope went home for lunch. Brutus met her at the door and sniffed her carefully to find out where she'd been and what animals she had interacted with. Then he got distracted by the sound of Jake dropping a plastic bag in the kitchen and ran off to investigate.

Penelope raised her voice to warn Jake. "Incoming!" She followed the dog, arriving in time to see Jake retrieving a block of still-wrapped cheese from the mastiff's jaws. He looked it over. "Didn't even have a chance to break the seal. I win."

Brutus sighed and went into the living room to throw himself on the couch.

Jake put the package down on the counter. "Grilled cheese, ham, and tomato sound good to you? I'll even heat up the leftover broccoli and we can pretend we eat like adults."

"Sounds great." Penelope got out the rest of the ingredients while he put the skillet on the stove. The cheese had indentations from Brutus's canine teeth. "Any news?"

"Your theory may hold water. Esther didn't have the current numbers for all the categories, but I looked at the matrix they're using. One input is the serious crime rate. The north site was already close to being knocked out because of transportation issues. I think the arsons will be enough to disqualify it completely." Butter sizzled in the pan.

"And how does that change things with the committee?" The cheese had suffered no ill effects from its recent peril. Penelope sliced another piece to replace the one she'd eaten.

"Esther wasn't completely certain, but she thinks it might be an even split. Which makes the Gardener of the Year the tiebreaker, and actually gives us a real motive for everything." He sliced four pieces of ham on the other end of the cutting board.

"That's great! Now all we need to do is figure out who benefits and maybe we'll know where the dogs are." Penelope checked the time. "In the next three hours."

Jake assembled sandwiches. "Yeah. The deadline is a problem. If we don't get the dogs back in time before the final scores are tallied…"

"Then the wrong person gets awarded the title. And even if the dogs are returned, the judges aren't likely to kick up a fuss afterward if whoever took them is still out there and nobody knows who it is."

Jake nodded and transferred the sandwiches to the skillet. "Right. If we can't stop it from happening in the first place, we're probably going to have to get enough evidence for legal proof. That's going to be a challenge, especially if the dogs have been returned in the meantime."

"Any luck with property records?"

"Waiting on a call back."

Penelope sat at the table and regarded him as he stood at the stove, spatula in hand. She couldn't quite keep the glee out of her voice. "It's going to kill Purcell if we figure out who burned all those cars before his detectives do." The current police chief had forced Jake into retirement. Worse, the man didn't like dogs.

Jake glanced over. "We haven't solved anything yet." Then his lips twitched. "But the thought has occurred to me."

"All because nobody considered the missing dogs important enough to investigate." Penelope shook her head. "That never would have happened when you were in charge."

Jake gave her a pained look. "Only because you'd have given me no peace. I don't think I can really claim the moral high ground on this one." He turned back to the skillet and flipped the sandwiches.

"Okay, but you were smart enough to fall into my clutches." Remembering the broccoli, Penelope got up and opened the refrigerator. "*He* would never attract someone of my caliber."

"The way I remember it, I found you, but I'll accept the argument."

Penelope found the container huddling in the very back with all the other discarded vegetables. "Isolde is certainly never going to let him forget." She cracked the lid and started the microwave. "Speaking of Isolde…"

"She and Carol are waiting for a call from animal control so they can go pick up their dogs. I think we can expect more baked goods to show up on our doorstep. From Carol, anyhow. I'm not sure Isolde is the baking type, though it wouldn't surprise me if she commissioned something from a bakery on top of everything else."

Isolde was far too proud to just ask for a favor. "You said something about not accepting money since you aren't a licensed private investigator."

"I'm keeping track of the hours we spend on this, and she's making a donation to the county shelter based on that. It means she'll get the tax write-off instead of us, but…"

Penelope moved behind him and wrapped her arms around his torso. "You're a good man, Jake Wheeler." She sat down again while he flipped the sandwiches in the skillet. "How hard is it going to be to get licensed?"

The look he shot her was almost guilty. "How did you know I was looking?"

"Because I know you." In truth, she'd been expecting him to latch onto something earlier. Unlike Penelope, Jake needed to have concrete goals. He'd enjoyed automating the accounting for her pet sitting business, and he had no problem helping her care for pets when she had more clients than she could handle, but he derived satisfaction from projects that had a distinct end point. Private investigation would fulfill that need, and it would use the skills he'd spent a lifetime developing.

"There's a fee, and a test. But my time on the force means I can skip the apprenticeship, so at least I wouldn't have to waste four years following cheating spouses around for someone else's business." He used the spatula to poke at the skillet. "I'm still not sure it makes sense to do. From a monetary standpoint, anyhow. I don't want to take divorce cases. There might be some business clients, for background checks and that sort of thing, but probably not many. And realistically, how many cases of kidnapped dogs are likely to come up?"

"But it would still be cheaper than a mid-life crisis corvette, right?" Penelope waited until Jake huffed a laugh and nodded. "So forget the money, for now. Is it something you would enjoy doing?" That was a safe question. She already knew the answer.

"I think so."

"Then you should look into it. We have your retirement income, plus what I make. If you have a business that loses money for a few years while you're getting started, we're not going to end up on the streets using Brutus to help beg for money." She stopped as she thought about it. "Though Brutus probably would be pretty good at it. He always looks hungry even when he's just eaten." She stopped as Jake started laughing. "Sorry, got sidetracked."

"You wouldn't be you if you didn't." He plated the grilled sandwiches and brought them over to the table. "But I'll think about it."

That last sentence meant he'd already decided to do it, but needed time to get all the information together so he could believe he'd arrived at a logical conclusion. Penelope just wasn't sure if *he* knew that.

Jake's phone rang just as he sat down. "Ah, property records." He answered the phone while he was taking out his notebook. "Hey, that was quick."

Penelope gave up trying to read his handwriting upside-down. Remembering the broccoli in the microwave, she retrieved the container, then served herself what she wanted and put the rest on Jake's plate. There was no point in saving any. If they didn't eat it now, it would go bad.

She had eaten half her sandwich when he finally hung up. "It sounds like you got something interesting."

"Yes. Well, maybe." He turned to his temporarily abandoned plate, then stopped when he noticed the mound of broccoli. "Is this retaliation for making Heidi expect a faster pace?"

"No. I'm just trying to mitigate the damage for all the fast food you're going to eat on stakeouts while working as a private investigator."

"Television shows might have given you a skewed image of what the work entails."

"Maybe. But we also needed to get rid of it, and you know garlic gives Brutus gas."

Jake looked doubtful. "I think the gas is a constant. The

garlic just makes it more noticeable." He shrugged. "Anyhow, not much on the downtown site. The lot and most of the buildings around it are owned by the same three companies that own most of the commercial real estate in that area."

Penelope frowned. "And if they really wanted to affect the decision, they'd just pay off a few people on the city council." Her history with the town's governing body had taught her a lot. The reward would be less blatant than outright bribes, but that would be the end result. "Tell me the east site gives us something."

Jake shoveled some of the broccoli onto her plate. "Something, though I'm not sure what. The site itself is owned by the same company that owns the downtown lot, so nothing there."

"But...?"

"But all the vacant buildings in the area were bought about three months ago by one company, CMI Commercial Holdings. They don't own property anywhere else in the city, and the company itself didn't exist last year."

"Who owns CMI?"

"From what we can tell, it's an LLC set up in Delaware with an anonymous trust as the beneficiary."

Penelope blinked. "It's sexy when you talk terms I don't understand at all."

He grinned and translated. "It's a shell company. There's no easy way to tell who owns it."

Penelope frowned and sat back. "Darn. I was hoping this would give us somewhere to look."

"It suggests we're on the right track, though. Someone has gone to a lot of trouble to hide their ownership. And they've made a pretty significant investment, especially if this is someone local and not a national company. If the east site is chosen, they'll make a killing. But if it isn't..."

Penelope nodded. "Might be worth burning a few cars to

make that happen." She thought about it as she ate her way through the tower of broccoli on her plate. "But it seems like there would be easier ways to make money."

"My guess would be it's more about not *losing* money at this point." Jake took another bite and paused. "I've seen this sort of thing too many times to count. Someone has a great idea to get rich. And it can't possibly lose money, so they invest everything. Sometimes they even get all their friends and family to invest their savings as well."

Penelope sighed. "And thus multi level marketing claims another victim." She'd had more than one burgeoning friendship implode when she refused to go to a presentation on whatever containers or supplements or beauty products were being sold.

"Except in this case, it's just real estate. And in the beginning, everyone has pure intentions. Naïve, but pure. But what seemed like a sure thing three months ago suddenly gets a little more shaky, and now there's a very real possibility that they own all this real estate that is going to be hard to unload. Then they panic and start making stupid decisions."

"Like burning cars and stealing dogs." Penelope speared the last bit of broccoli. "So maybe we know *why*, but we still don't know *who*."

"Right."

They sat in silence for a moment. Finally, Jake put his fork down. "What I keep coming back to is whoever stole the dogs knew exactly who the judges were. That has to help us. Who would know that?"

"Not Tamsin and Leo, though I can absolutely see them in a harebrained real estate scheme that involves torching cars to make money. But I'd be surprised if they could raise any money at this point, so I think they'd fail before they got started."

Jake nodded. "Right. I think we can rule them out. If they had been involved in taking the first group of dogs, they would have taken Guinevere at the start, not two days later. Who else?"

"The judges themselves."

"Yes. But we know they couldn't have taken the dogs unless they're working with someone else. Which they could be, I guess." Jake eyed the remaining broccoli on his plate. "I give up on this. Brutus!"

The couch creaked, then settled with a thud. The mastiff rounded the corner two seconds later and went straight to the plate Jake had put on the ground.

"Anyone who saw them meeting. Janitors…" Penelope stopped. "Do you know where they had their meetings? I know one was at the library after the general meeting on Wednesday night, but they must have had a meeting before then." Meeting in person might not have been necessary, but Penelope suspected some of the judges were not as tied to email as others. Going over the rules and making sure the judging was somewhat consistent probably meant they had to get together at least a few times.

"I'll find out."

While Jake was making calls, Penelope picked up the plate from the floor and cleaned up the kitchen. Jake joined her a few moments later. "Other than the Wednesday night meeting, everything was at Jillian and Bill's house." He took the skillet from her and dried it. "And guess who else was there."

Penelope raised her eyebrows and waited.

"Rufus Tinsdale. He was spreading the mulch the Smiths had just gotten delivered."

Penelope thought about the sullen man who had stayed quiet while his mother did the talking. She didn't have a good sense of him at all. "The same Rufus who might have spread something smelling of fish on Esther's yard? We should go talk to him."

"Yes. Though first we have to figure out where he is." He put the skillet away and closed the cabinet door. "We have the business address, but it's Sunday. There won't be anyone there."

Penelope dried her hands. "Yes, but his mother entered the festival competition this year. Her home address is online. She'll know how to get in touch with him." She grinned at him. "See? Having the list available for everyone is convenient."

Jake shook his head. "La la la, I can't hear you." He held up his key chain. "Shall we?"

CHAPTER 26

*R*ebecca Tinsdale lived in an older ranch-style house next to a sunflower field on the south edge of town. An enormous oak tree dominated one side of the yard, with huge boulders forming a tableau on the other side of the driveway. Flowers grew from the natural crevices in the rocks. The whole thing looked easy to maintain and had an air of permanence that Penelope appreciated, though she suspected the house was in no danger of winning the festival contest.

The sound of their car wheels on gravel brought Rebecca to the door, and she waved. An ancient yellow lab raised his head from the dirt, and then let it fall back down when Jake and Penelope got out. Apparently, they didn't look like a threat. Penelope had half-expected to hear a chorus of small dogs, but the only noise came from leaves rattling in the breeze.

"Jake and Penelope, right?" Jeans, a company t-shirt, and work boots appeared to be Rebecca's standard attire, at work or home. "What can I do for you?"

Jake took the lead. "We're trying to get in touch with

Rufus to ask him a couple of things. Can you give us his address?"

"He lives here, but he's away at the moment. I can give you his number, but he isn't answering it this afternoon." Rebecca paused. "Or, at least, he isn't answering it when I call him. Is there something I can help you with?"

Penelope noted the tight muscles around Rebecca's eyes. She was doing a good job of acting as if nothing was wrong, yet her face said she was worried. But was she worried because she was involved in something shady and people were asking questions, or because she was afraid of what her son might have done? Penelope decided to trust her instinct. "We wanted to ask Rufus about the missing dogs."

Rebecca closed her eyes for a full second. When she opened them, she let out a breath. "I knew he was mixed up in something he shouldn't be. You'd better come in."

Penelope followed her into the house to the kitchen. The sturdiness she'd felt in the landscaping permeated the interior, with its heavy appliances and comfortable furniture. A plaque reading *Bless This Mess* held hooks with at least ten sets of keys.

"You want something to drink?" Rebecca sighed. "I'm having a beer."

Penelope joined her, while Jake declined.

When they were all seated at the trestle table in the kitchen, Rebecca opened her drink. "Okay, rip the bandaid off. What's going on?"

Jake gave an admirably concise summary of their thoughts about the motive behind the missing dogs and the judging, mentioning the real estate and the shell corporation. "We don't have any proof at all that Rufus is involved," he admitted, "but he's one of the few people in town who knows who the judges are."

Rebecca nodded slowly. "This helps put a few pieces

together." Her eyes went to a stack of open envelopes in a tray next to the door. "Last week, I found out someone had taken out a loan against the business. I thought it was one of those identity theft things, and I was all ready to call the police, but..." Her mouth twisted. "Do you have children?"

"I do," Penelope said.

"Then you know how it is. They can hide things from you, but their reactions give them away in the end."

Penelope nodded. Growing up, Seth rarely got into trouble, or at least rarely got caught. But he had one particular look Penelope had learned meant she needed to start asking questions.

"All I could get out of him was there was some amazing opportunity, that he would return double the amount soon, and that I just needed to trust him." Rebecca shook her head. "As if signing my name to a loan was a great way to gain trust." Her voice took on a note of disbelief. "He even tried to get me to take another loan out, to 'double our investment' so we could get even more money back."

Penelope tried to keep the grimace off her face. "Sounds like someone is conning him."

"I have no doubt about that, though I can't get that through his head. He just tells me I'm thinking too small and that I'll see when he makes us rich." She threw up her hands. "Why would I want to be rich? I enjoy what I do."

Rebecca's philosophy agreed with Penelope's. She nodded. "Why mess up a good thing?"

"Right? The house is paid for, the business is doing well — or at least it was before some idiot took out a loan at a ridiculous interest rate. I've met a lot of rich people, and none of them were happy. But ever since Rufus took up with those people at the community college, it's all about 'being an entrepreneur means this' and 'the business should be growing' and nothing I say makes any difference."

Jake leaned forward before Penelope could commiserate about people who had never run a business offering 'expert' advice to people who had successfully started their own. "Which people at the community college? Do you know their names?"

Rebecca shook her head. "I never met them, and he stopped talking about them around me after I started asking questions." She glanced around the kitchen. "I don't know where I went wrong. This place is nothing to be ashamed about." She shook her head sharply. "Don't mind me. I think one girl was named Linda, or something like that. And I'm pretty sure one of them was teaching the class."

"Do you know which class?"

"It had to be either English or chemistry. Those are the only two classes he was taking. And he might have dropped the chemistry class."

Penelope met Jake's eye. They knew an English professor at the local community college. And Penelope didn't like the man, so she was more than willing to investigate him.

Jake looked at his notebook. "One last thing. Do you know where Rufus was Wednesday evening?"

"He was here with me." Rebecca nodded at the oak tree visible through the kitchen window. "I was worried one of the limbs would come down and hit the house during the storm, so he was up in the oak, trimming branches right up until it got too windy for it to be safe. It's the same every year — work gets so busy before the festival that I don't have time to take care of things at home. That's one reason it took me so long to find out about the loan. Anyhow, after that we came in to eat, and then we went out together in the truck and worked on keeping the roads around here clear. He was with me until at least three in the morning."

Penelope checked with Jake and finished her beer. "Thank you. That helps a lot."

Jake nodded. "Ask Rufus to give us a call when he gets home."

Rebecca walked them to the front door. "How much trouble is he in?"

Jake's face was neutral. "That depends on how much he's been involved. It's possible he just passed along some information, in which case his only real crime would be the loan he took out in your name. If he's had a more active role..." He shrugged. "If he has, get him a good lawyer and make sure he's the first one to cut a deal."

Rebecca nodded once. "I appreciate you stopping by."

The old yellow lab ambled into the house as they left.

CHAPTER 27

Jake backed slowly down the gravel drive to the main road, then drove half a mile, pulled over to the curb, and shut the engine off. "So…"

"Iain Hotz. It has to be." Penelope turned sideways in her seat to face him. "Except he had an alibi for the time the dogs were stolen, didn't he?"

Jake flipped back through his notes. "Linnea Kowalcik said he was there."

"It's hard to imagine her lying for him." Penelope grimaced. "Those two are just barely on speaking terms. I've heard them yelling at each other at the dog park more than once."

"He spent half the time we were in the beer tent complaining about her. Apparently she didn't take his class seriously enough, and he didn't appreciate that."

Penelope relayed the story about Linnea's Pinocchio bondage essay. "I think that's why he feels she wasn't taking his class seriously. Though *she* said he gave her the highest score in the class. I got the feeling he liked the essay."

"Maybe he figured out she was making fun of him after he turned in the grades," Jake said.

"Yeah…" Penelope let her voice trail off as she thought. "Except."

Jake waited patiently.

"Do we have any other confirmation that Iain was there during the entire meeting? Other than Linnea, I mean."

Jake flipped the page on his notes. "No. But that holds true for almost everyone there. Most people really weren't paying attention to who was around them."

"Okay. So you might think I'm stretching things…"

Jake's lips twitched. "Go ahead."

"The last time I saw Iain and Linnea together at the dog park, they were yelling at each other. It was the usual thing, about him bringing his big dog into the little dog section."

Jake nodded. He had listened to her dog park stories for years and had even taken a few dogs there himself. Dog park drama came up in conversation between them at least once per week.

"I don't know if you've ever seen Linnea's dog. Britta is one of those chihuahuas who barks at every other dog at the dog park. If she got into the big dog side, she'd probably have them backed up against the fence peeing on themselves."

Jake nodded again. "I haven't met Britta the chihuahua, but I know her in spirit."

"Right. But while Linnea and Iain were yelling, Britta and Iain's dog, Barnaby, were lying down in the grass next to each other. Like they spent a lot of time together." Penelope shrugged. "Maybe Britta just likes Barnaby for some reason."

Jake started the car. "I'd hate to take that to a judge to get a search warrant, but that's not my problem anymore. I think we should take a closer look at Iain. Is his contact info on the website?"

"Of course it is." Penelope brought up the page on her phone and read the address to him.

Jake pulled the car in a u-turn and accelerated to merge into traffic. He saw her checking the clock on the dashboard. "Assuming the dogs are being kept at someone's house, we may still have time to get them back before the judging. We can at least check out where both Iain and Linnea live before the ceremony."

"Assuming there isn't someone in on this aside from Iain, Linnea, and Rufus," Penelope said.

"Right. If there are more people involved, or the dogs just aren't there, we'll have to track down Rufus and try to get him to talk. He seems like the weakest link."

Penelope rubbed sweaty palms on her thighs. "I just don't want them to panic and dump the dogs somewhere. Or worse."

Jake reached over and took her hand. "I'm pretty sure they'll all be concentrating on the contest results for the next few hours. This is our best chance to find the dogs." He pulled over to the curb in a neighborhood of neo-Tudor monstrosities on lots far too small for that amount of house. "That's his place up there."

Penelope looked. Iain's house blended into the sea of beige stucco around it. A line of neatly pruned red roses stood in the narrow front yard, with a tiny white picket fence marching around the border. The fence provided more of a visual element than any real barrier. Brutus would have walked right over it.

No car waited in the driveway, but the garage door was closed. Iain could still be inside. "Are we going to come straight out and ask him if he's behind the shell company, or do you have a better plan?"

"I was going to play it by ear. Maybe ask if he's heard

anything about the missing dogs." Jake opened his door. "Ready?"

Penelope met him on the sidewalk and held his hand as they walked to Iain's door. "If you become a private investigator, are you going to get a bunch of disguises? Maybe a tuxedo? I have some thoughts."

"I'd be shocked if you didn't," he said. "If I ever have a case that requires a tuxedo, I'll be sure to let you know."

They walked up the driveway to the house. An envelope had been taped to the front door. Penelope read the return address as she reached for the doorbell. "Uh oh. Someone's in trouble with their homeowners' association." Ignoring the doorbell, she freed the envelope and opened the unglued flap.

Jake shifted so her actions wouldn't be seen by anyone watching from the street. "You, of all people, should know that tampering with mail is a federal offense."

"I do. But this isn't mail. This is just a piece of paper taped on someone's front door. I don't think there's a law against this."

"You know there's a difference between something actually being legal and not knowing that it isn't, right?"

Penelope ignored him and unfolded the paper. "Well, look at that. Someone ratted Iain out to the HOA because he has too many dogs on the property." She put the paper back in the envelope and pressed the tape against the door again. It sagged, ready to fall off at the first hint of a breeze. "This is very interesting, because I saw him at the dog park just a few days ago, and he only had one dog at that point." Penelope pushed the doorbell eight times in quick succession.

A chorus of yapping sounded from behind the door. Aside from one deeper bark, all were high pitched.

Penelope looked over at Jake. They smiled at each other. "Imagine that," she said.

"That certainly does sound like more than one dog."

A window from the house next door slammed shut. Penelope glanced over. "And I think we know who complained to the homeowner association." Lifting the doormat disturbed a conclave of earwigs, but didn't reveal a key. There weren't any planters near the door. She pulled her backpack around and started rummaging through the front pocket. "Hang on. They're in here somewhere."

"What are?"

"My lock picks." Under four sets of keys, she finally found them. "Aha! Distract anyone who starts looking." Penelope knelt in front of the door.

Jake rubbed his forehead. "Really? The *front* door?"

"Oh yeah, the back patio doors on the houses in this neighborhood had really cheap locks when they were installed, and they all broke within a year. Everyone has broom handles in the track. Lock picks won't help with that."

Jake turned away from her, took out his notebook, and leaned against the wall, shielding Penelope from view of the street and looking like he was writing a note to leave on Iain's door. "Some people must just get the lock fixed."

Penelope inserted the tension wrench. "A lot of people tried. But the size of the lock on the patio door is not standard. I assume the idea was to force people to buy replacements from the same company that made the doors. And then they went out of business. To fix them now would require replacing the entire door, and that's a non-standard size, too." She stopped talking and inserted the hook pick. Someone with more experience might be able to carry on a conversation at the same time, but she needed all her concentration on what she was doing.

A car horn in the street in front of the house made her drop the hook pick. "Dang it." She kept the tension wrench in place and stretched to reach where it had fallen. "Someday I'm going to be good at this."

Jake crouched to tie his shoe and cleared his throat. "Honey, you know I love you and support you in all your endeavors, right?" He stood up again.

Penelope rested her head against the door. "You're right. You should do this. You're faster." She stood up and offered the lock picks.

He held up a key. "I thought maybe we'd try this instead."

Penelope frowned at him. "Where'd you find that?"

He motioned to the closest patch of dirt where he'd crouched down. "In the sprinkler controller."

Penelope sighed and put her lock picks away.

"You'll get there. You just need a little more practice." Jake unlocked the door. He paused. "I never thought I'd be telling someone to practice lock picking, but here we are."

"Exactly. And for the record, the sprinkler controller is a really antisocial place to store the spare key."

Jake eased the door open. A grey and golden muzzle immediately pushed into the gap.

Penelope pulled a treat from her pocket. "Hi, Barnaby!" She gave the golden retriever the treat as Jake opened the door wider.

By the time they had stepped inside and closed the door behind them, Barnaby was wagging his tail and bouncing up and down on his front legs. Penelope spent a moment petting him and scratching his rear, feeding him a few more treats while she was at it. Then she stood and looked around.

"He really bought into the whole professor thing, didn't he?" Brown leather couches took up the space between tall bookshelves. Most of the shelves held hardback versions of novels Penelope recognized as classics but hadn't read.

Back when Seth had been young, and she'd been desperate for adult company, she'd made three attempts to get through *Gravity's Rainbow* for a book club and finally gave up. Then the club had chosen James Joyce's *Ulysses* for the next month, so she'd joined a movie review group instead. Even if she didn't enjoy a film, it only took an hour or two.

Iain had *Gravity's Rainbow* and *Ulysses* on either side of *Infinite Jest*. Penelope hadn't read the third one either; given its company, she added it to her mental list of books to avoid. Iain's novels looked well read, though she noticed there weren't any books that looked as if they had recently been set down. The room had the casual disarray that came from everyday living, so she didn't think he had picked up in expectation of company. Maybe he'd switched to ebooks.

Another bookshelf held different whiskeys, but the crystal glasses were covered in a fine layer of dust. The open wall space was taken up by reproductions of French impressionists. The whole area seemed more like a set for a play than a living space.

A broom handle lay in the track of the sliding glass door.

The only note that didn't fit was the sour smell of dog urine and a stronger smell of feces.

A staircase went up to the second floor, which presumably held the master bedroom and bath, but Penelope followed Jake to a closed door at the edge of the living room. When they cracked the door, frenzied barking and stronger smells assaulted them.

The good news was all four dogs were alive and reasonably healthy. Piggins stood on the corner of the bed, barking at them in all his Bichon frise glory. The fur on his ears was crusted with something dark, but his eyes were bright. Briar, the dachshund, ran forward, barked, then ran under the bed, out the other side, and barked at them from the far side of the room. The other two missing dogs, Jimmy and ZigZig, yapped ferociously while backing away.

If the four dogs had been making that amount of noise since Wednesday night, Penelope wasn't surprised the neighbors had complained. And that was with the windows closed — she suspected Iain had kept the windows open as much as possible.

The space had originally been a guest bedroom, from the looks of things, but after five days housing four little dogs, Penelope was pretty sure it was going to need a tear-down remodel. A large pee pad had been placed in the corner, but it appeared to have been ignored by the dogs in favor of carpet and the bed. The remains of a pair of slippers littered the room. The water bowl by the door was nearly empty, and at least one dog had suffered from diarrhea since the last time Iain had cleaned.

Jake pulled the door closed. "Now we need to decide what to do. We could either lock everything up again and call the police and give them some story about seeing something through the window, or we could just take the dogs with us."

Penelope absently petted the golden retriever by her side and fed him another treat. "If we involve the police, we'd have time to let everyone know the dogs were found, but we'd probably be stuck here for the next few hours and miss the judging."

"Yes. Also, someone might not believe our story that we just happened to notice something while standing around outside. We *could* get charged with breaking and entering."

Penelope met his gaze. In a perfect world, that wouldn't be a worry, but given how Chief Purcell felt about the two of them, it was a distinct possibility. "That probably won't look so good on your application for a private investigator's license."

"On the plus side, I would save a lot of money on application fees."

Penelope shrugged. "Sounds like we have our answer. I'm

going to go get crates and leashes out of the car." They kept the emergency car supplies in two small dog crates. Penelope had used the crates multiple times to hold stray dogs and cats she'd picked up by the side of the road, and never once used the emergency supplies. Jake had vetoed her suggestion of getting rid of the extra bottled water in favor of another dog crate.

"While you're doing that, I'm going to take some pictures. We may need to prove this is where we got them if Iain doesn't get charged with something else from this whole mess."

Spurred on by the worry that Iain might come home for something before heading to the awards ceremony, Penelope slipped out the door without letting Barnaby follow, jogged to the car, and jogged back with both crates and two leashes.

The curtains twitched on the house next door. Penelope thought anyone at the point of complaining to the homeowners' association about their neighbor was unlikely to call up the same neighbor to tell him it looked like someone was stealing the dogs causing the problem, but she didn't want to test that theory. She hurried back inside, where Jake was just standing at the guest room doorway, taking pictures of the room and the snapping dogs.

He closed the door again as she returned his car keys. "Can you get the dogs ready to go? I want to check the rest of the house."

Penelope nodded. There wasn't room for two people to chase the dogs around in the room anyhow. "Five minutes? This whole thing is making me nervous."

He smiled. "Five minutes."

That left Penelope trying to get control over four smelly dogs who didn't know her at all. Briar, Jillian and Bill's dachshund, turned out to be the easiest. Penelope held up a treat, tossed it into the first open crate, and then closed the door after the dog went in.

The other three were a little more difficult, mostly because Penelope didn't want to go into the room and get dog poop all over her shoes. When all this was over, Iain would need to rip out the carpet and possibly the underlying floorboards. It served him right.

Barnaby, the golden retriever who normally was the sole canine occupant, stood near the door and wagged his tail. Every few minutes Penelope gave him another treat just so he wouldn't feel left out.

Jake jogged down the stairs as she was working on the last hold-out. ZigZig still wore his harness, proudly proclaiming Laurence's favorite football team. Penelope tossed a towel from the bathroom over him, clipped the leash on, and let go. By the time he had worked his way out from under the towel, he forgot he was trying to bite her.

"One more thing," Jake said as he went to the door leading to the garage. Penelope noticed he was using a paper towel to touch the surface. At least one of them had remembered not to leave fingerprints all over the place. She wiped down the door knob and frame with the towel she'd used to catch ZigZig, only noticing afterward that she had smeared a bit of dog poop around. If this had been a client's house, she would have hurried to clean it. As it was, she figured Iain deserved that as well. What kind of idiot threw four stolen dogs into a single room together like that?

With a carrier and leash in each hand, Penelope made her way to the front door. Barnaby danced around in joy, clearly thinking they were all going on a walk together. "He doesn't deserve a dog as nice as you," Penelope said, putting down the carriers so she could toss another treat to the golden retriever. She raised her voice. "Two more minutes and I'm leaving you here."

"Only if you're walking," he called back. "You haven't had lessons on how to hot-wire a car yet." But he was closing the door to the garage and walking toward her even as he said it.

Penelope let him take two of the dogs. "Do you really know how to hot-wire a car?"

He raised one eyebrow. "Why do I get the feeling you're far more attracted by my ability to commit crime than you ever were by my career in stopping it?" He wiped the door handle, inside and out, and then held the door open so she could pass through.

"Of course I am. Think of the possibilities." She leaned over to kiss him as she maneuvered her charges through the opening. "But how many men would think to hold the door for their wife as they're in the middle of a burglary? I'll keep you even if you can't hot-wire a car."

"That's good, because my knowledge is more theoretical than practical. *And* it involves first finding a car that is more than forty years old." He followed her out the door. ZigZig had decided he wanted to stay so he could growl at Barnaby for a while, but Jake tugged on the leash until the little dog had moved past the threshold. Penelope tossed another treat through the crack for the still-hopeful Barnaby before Jake pulled the door shut.

Back in the car, idling with all the windows rolled down and the fan blowing fresh air in their faces, Penelope took a deep breath and let it out slowly. The dogs waited quietly for the car to start moving. "I don't know if I'm ready for a life of crime. You need to have nerves of steel for that sort of thing."

Jake kept a straight face, but she could tell it was an effort. "You did great for your first time. But I'd understand if you cut your dog theft career short."

"I think I just need more practice." Penelope laughed when Jake closed his eyes. "Never mind. What now?"

Jake glanced at the dashboard. "There's no time to drop

them off at their houses. I think we just take them straight to the judging meeting." He pulled away from the curb.

Penelope relaxed as they left the street with Iain's house. "Did you find anything upstairs?"

"A contract for a remodel of one of the vacant businesses by the east site. They're turning it into a fried chicken restaurant."

"Signed by Iain?"

"And Linnea."

Penelope shook her head. "With everything they're doing to make people think they hate each other, they *have* to be having an affair." She thought about it. "I bet it started when she was a student in his class. He seems like one of those guys." She shook her head. "What were you looking for out in the garage?"

The car accelerated to make it through a yellow light. "Anything that might suggest he's the arsonist. But I didn't even see a gas can."

"It could still be him. He could have it in his car." If the arsonist wasn't Iain, then Linnea or Rufus would be the main suspects. Penelope really didn't want Rufus to be the arsonist, just for Rebecca's sake. Though presumably Iain was someone's son as well. At least Penelope didn't know Iain's mother.

"It could be a lot of people. But you're right, absence of evidence isn't evidence of absence."

"I love it when you talk dirty."

Jake grinned and pulled up next to the red curb near the library meeting rooms. After putting the car in park, he tapped on his phone and lifted it to his ear. "Jillian? Are you in the meeting room at the library? Great. We're outside with the dogs. Can you let Laurence, Connie, and Josie know as well? What?" He paused to listen, then rolled his eyes. "Yes, I mean, if they just happen to be in the judges' room with you." He hung up. "This whole town is insane."

"That's why you love it so much." Penelope got out and unloaded the carriers, just in time for Josie to burst out a door and run across the lawn to them.

"Piggins!"

When Penelope let go of the leash, the Bichon nearly levitated across the distance to greet her. After that, there was ten minutes of joyful chaos as the dogs were reunited with their owners. Jillian sent Bill off with instructions to drive home and return with Briar's medication, but she wasn't willing to let him take their dog out of her sight.

ZigZig growled at everyone, including Laurence, though his owner hugged him anyhow. Penelope worried the man was about to lose an ear, but ZigZig just licked him.

Josie finally stopped focusing on Piggins long enough to thank Jake and Penelope. "But who had them?"

Penelope glanced at Jake. If word got out that Iain had taken the dogs, everyone would know Jake and Penelope had broken into his house to get them back. "Maybe it would be better to get into that later."

Finally Jillian cleared her throat and straightened, Briar still firmly in her arms. "Judges! We still have decisions to make. Let's go back inside and finish up."

The parking enforcement golf cart that had been speeding toward them suddenly turned down one of the other rows of cars, as if there might be something more important to check out among the free parking than a car apparently parked in the labeled fire lane. Jake might no longer be the assistant police chief, but many of his former employees seemed to forget that on occasion. He swung his keys into his palm. "We need to go find a place to park anyhow."

After piling the empty crates in the car, Penelope hopped

in and fastened her seatbelt. "Congratulations on solving your first case! Isolde will be pleased."

Jake pulled away from the curb and then exchanged waves with the middle-aged woman driving the parking enforcement cart. "I'm not sure Isolde is going to be pleased about much, today." He handed his phone to her. "Look what animal control just sent to me."

Penelope looked at the picture on the screen. Taken from a high angle in a dusty lobby, it showed the back of a woman wearing scrubs who stood behind a reception desk. The image had a timestamp from late Friday morning. Although it had clearly been set up to monitor the movements of the employee dealing with cash payments, it still caught an image of the two people holding pet carriers on the other side of the desk. Penelope recognized Tamsin and Leo. "I guess they tracked down the person who knew how to access the security system."

"I don't know if Carol will want to press charges, but at least this is enough evidence for Isolde to change some things. Tamsin and Leo might have to stop opening businesses and start working for one instead."

Penelope put Jake's phone down on the center console. "Do you know if Isolde has seen it yet?"

He pulled into the last available parking spot on the row. "Let's go find out."

CHAPTER 28

For the last day of the festival, tickets had been discounted, food prices had been lowered, and some booths had sold out of prizes and closed early. Penelope bought cotton candy before she and Jake went over to the presentation area near the beer tent. The crew working the final day had erected a small platform with a stepladder next to it for easy access.

Penelope eyed the extension cords chained together as she ate a tuft of cotton candy. "Somehow I think the fire marshal hasn't seen this one yet."

Jake blinked and gave a deep sigh. "It only has to last for an hour or so." He said it to her, but Penelope was fairly certain his words had been meant for himself. While Penelope saw shoddy work and planned around it, Jake felt attacked and had to restrain himself from taking charge. "Beer?"

"If nobody drinks what's left in the keg, it's going to go bad." Penelope offered her cotton candy to him. "But if we drink it, it's pure profit for the festival. So really, drinking beer is just the neighborly thing to do." Plus, it would get them a seat in the shade.

"We wouldn't want to be rude."

The teenager monitoring the entrance waved them through without checking their IDs. Jake held Penelope's elbow and kept moving when she would have stopped. "Just accept it."

"Are you saying I can't pass for a twenty-year-old anymore?" She pulled off another tuft from the cotton candy.

"Why would you want to?" He let go of her elbow. "You're like a fine wine. You just get better with age."

"Nice save, Slick." Penelope scanned the tables. "I'll grab seats if you get the drinks."

Borrowing a towel from a volunteer studying with a textbook in the corner, Penelope cleared a table and wiped it off. There were fewer people than she'd been expecting for the final awards ceremony. Every other year she'd been there, the beer tent had been overcapacity, and the folding chairs in neat rows on the nearby lawn had all been in use. This time, most of the seats were empty, and there were still tables with a good view in the tent. Penelope wondered if they had shown up at the wrong time.

Jake offered an explanation when he came with two cups of beer a few minutes later. "The freezer at Rosa's Cantina failed, so they're trying to use up all the frozen meat before it goes bad. Five tacos for a dollar, and happy hour prices for alcohol. I think attendance might be a little low for the ceremony." He tilted his head toward the other side of the tent. "But Iain's in charge of the volunteers in here again this afternoon, so at least we know he won't duck out to go home."

A man in his thirties, whom Penelope recognized as the most junior city council member, jumped onto the platform. Then he froze and held his arms out to balance like a surfer, waiting for the platform to finish swaying. Jake's hand tightened on his beer.

Once he could stand straight again, the man switched on the microphone. He winced as it squealed. The group seated near the speakers covered their ears. "Good afternoon, everyone! Welcome to the Rose Garden Society Festival awards program. I'm Councilman Rory Nestor, from district three. Quite a few familiar faces out there. It's good to see so many of you."

He paused and looked out at the nearly empty seating. "Uh, I guess maybe a lot of people went to get tacos." It was a clear deviation from a scripted speech. Having done some campaigning herself, Penelope felt a little sorry for him, but less sorry than she would have if she hadn't known he'd left his wife and twin infants for his campaign manager as soon as the election results had come in.

The sound system squealed again. "But we're going to go ahead anyhow." He consulted a piece of paper. "First off, we have Hilda Brophy to present the certificates to the rose garden volunteers who are celebrating anniversaries this year." He waited, looking around the area. "Hilda?" He squinted at the paper. "Or maybe Harry? Harry Brady?"

Esther rolled up to the table. "I thought I might find you two here."

Penelope greeted her. "We're drinking beer to help the local economy."

On the other side of the walkway, the platform wobbled again as the council member turned in a circle, clearly looking for someone heading toward the podium. Jake stood up and turned away from the sight. "I'll get you a drink."

Esther watched him walk away. "Do you think he can keep quiet, or is he going to end up as the construction supervisor for next year's festival?"

"I'm a little surprised he hasn't gone over to fix whatever they forgot to tighten yet. Who the heck is Hilda Brophy?"

"I believe that's supposed to read Hiram Brody. Rory's wife really did an excellent job covering up his difficulty reading when he was campaigning."

Penelope saw Hiram, a thin man in his nineties, shuffling toward the platform with his usual three-inch stride. Silver hair peaked out under the edges of his straw boater. At his current rate of travel, he would make it there in two minutes, which was probably about how long it would take the council member to figure out the correct name.

She was fairly certain Hiram couldn't climb the stepladder to get onto the podium. But with the way the podium shook every time Rory moved, having Hiram read the results from the ground seemed like a far better option. That would make this the first time Penelope applauded lack of access for the disabled.

Esther leaned forward. "And?"

Penelope matched her posture. "The dogs are back," she whispered. "We found them in Iain Hotz's house." With one eye on the other side of the tent to make sure Iain stayed over there, she recounted their afternoon to Esther.

After Penelope had finished, Esther gave a dark look toward the other side of the tent. "Never trust someone who only surrounds themselves with younger people."

"Right?" Penelope paused and eyed Esther. "Although, come to think of it, that would apply to you, too." Esther had reached an age where her peer group had started to disappear, or at least become less mobile.

Esther hooted. "You probably shouldn't trust me, either."

Jake came back and placed Esther's beer down. "Maybe we should have gone for tacos." Rory had jumped down from the podium and seemed to be preparing to boost Hiram up onto the platform. "Oh, god." Jake ducked under the beer tent tape, strode across the walkway, and grabbed the microphone stand, moving it down to the ground. By the time Hiram arrived, Jake had finished adjusting the height.

Esther glanced over at Penelope. "You found a good man with that one."

Penelope nodded, still looking at Jake. He stood waiting in the grass next to the podium, probably to forestall the next dangerous move. "No argument here." She turned back to Esther. "He's going to apply for a private investigator's license. I mean, he's still working through the pros and cons, but he'll apply."

Hiram tapped the microphone, setting off another round of audio feedback. "Good afternoon. I'm Hiram Brody." Turning around to glare at Rory took ten steps and fifteen seconds, then an equal amount of time to shuffle around to face the microphone again. "Volunteerism is the heart of the community, and like any heart, it takes many parts working together to keep the body alive."

Hiram had retired as an anatomy instructor thirty years before, but had never lost his love of teaching. Penelope had heard him speak many times and had been both entertained and enlightened by his presentations. Other people rolled their eyes when his name was mentioned. But everyone had strong opinions about his liver speech at the council meeting — the developer hadn't appreciated being cast in the role of the gallstone.

"The first stage in the volunteering journey is like the right atrium, where the lifeblood gathers from the rest of the body of the town. It's not a high pressure area, but it is important nonetheless. Our volunteers celebrating their first year with the Rose Garden Society are Diane Lavola..." He paused, waiting for the smattering of applause to die down before moving on to the next name. "Bret Wade..."

Esther leaned forward again. "I saw Isolde talking to Leo

and Tamsin a few minutes ago. From what I could hear, she's offering them a salary if they leave town and stay away for at least five years."

Penelope clapped for the name Hiram had just read. "Only Isolde would think to bring back the concept of the remittance man. Or woman." She frowned. "Were remittance women a thing, or was it just the men?"

Esther's look was a cross between fondness and exasperation. "I don't know for sure, but I'm guessing just men. Women weren't supposed to be moving off to new places by themselves at the time."

Penelope nodded. "Now we just ship the kids off to college and give them money to stay there, but I guess that's not quite the same thing." She gave a shake of her head, switching back to the important part of what Esther had said. "That must be hard for Isolde. They're her only relatives."

"She should have cut them off years ago. Knowing they were going to inherit the family fortune poisoned their approach to life. Isolde should have tied everything up in a trust back when they were in high school. They should just be glad she's letting them keep whatever they made from selling Guinevere's collar. Did you know that thing had actual diamonds on it?"

Penelope remembered how the dog's neck had glittered in the dim light. "Really? I'm surprised they didn't steal the collar before now."

"Too obvious. Tamsin and Leo are lazy, not stupid. They never think things through because they know she'll always be there to bail them out."

Penelope clapped for the next name. "Seth knows all he's likely to inherit from me are whatever animals I own when I die. Last I heard, his dad was on his third set of kids, and he was never that good with money to begin with, so Seth has been spared the curse of inherited wealth." She might have felt bad about not having anything to leave to her son, but he was doing just fine on his own. All those hours he'd spent playing video games growing up had somehow paid off.

She'd tried hard to maintain cordial relations with her ex-husband, wanting Seth to have a good relationship with his father. But eventually she realized she was doing more harm than good — to Seth, the only person who mattered — by forcing her ex to live up to more than the most basic promises. So she'd helped coach baseball, learned the right things to pack when hiking, and even taken them on one disastrously memorable fishing trip. As far as she knew, Seth and his father hadn't spoken beyond a quick call at Christmas for five years. Her son occasionally met up with his half-siblings when he was traveling.

Esther looked over at the podium. "It's too bad you didn't meet Jake thirty-five years earlier."

Penelope's laughter startled people near them and made Jake look over. "We would have hated each other. I was a very different person then." She waved to Jake and then turned back to Esther. "Out of everyone involved in this whole mess, I really only feel bad about Rebecca Tinsdale. Even if Rufus doesn't end up in jail after all this, she still has to do something about him. He stole a bunch of money from the business."

"Maybe he'll learn something from this experience," Esther said. She didn't sound very convinced. Penelope didn't hold out much hope, either. From what she'd seen, people who fell for get-rich-quick schemes went right to the next one after the previous one failed.

Up near the platform, Hiram had moved past the right ventricle — the volunteers who had stayed for five years — through the oxygenating lungs into the left atrium, and was now reading the names of people who were celebrating their ten-year anniversary.

Penelope tried to fix the path in her memory. "At least Hiram chose something easy this time. Were you there for the speech when he used the kidneys? I never did figure out the whole Loop of Henle thing." What she remembered most from that speech, another council meeting special, were the faces of the council members when they finally realized they'd been cast in the role of urine.

Esther shook her head. "I think I was on a bird-watching holiday when that one happened. His large intestine speech is still my favorite. You missed that one when you and Jake went backpacking."

Penelope had enjoyed that trip — five days with just the two of them, a whole lot of bugs, and amazing scenery — but she wished someone had recorded Hiram's speech at the public meeting of the hospital administrators. From all accounts, it had been a doozy.

"Where do you suppose the gotcha is in this one? And who?" Hiram never gave a speech that didn't have some dig at someone. Nobody would dare suggest he forego it, either, lest they be cast in the role of the disease or waste product.

Esther looked toward Hiram and then back at Penelope. "I think myocardial infarction must be coming up, and… He's a native organic, so there's a wide field to choose from."

They clapped for the final member of the left atrium.

Hiram surveyed the crowd. "And now, before we get to the pinnacle of the heart, the fifteen-year volunteers who make up the muscles of the left ventricle, we need to pause a moment to consider things that can go wrong. If the arteries that supply oxygen to the heart muscles themselves don't work, it can lead to a myocardial infarction, commonly known as a heart attack."

"You called it," Penelope said.

Hiram continued. "When that happens, the muscle cells of all four chambers can die. So remember how important it is to acknowledge your volunteers, and take the time to know their names, and pronounce them correctly." He stopped talking and began the slow shuffle to turn around and glare at Rory again.

Esther laughed quietly. Near the stage, Jake was rubbing his mouth with one hand, a sure sign he was having difficulty keeping a straight face.

Finally Hiram finished turning toward the microphone again. "We have two volunteers who are celebrating their fifteen-year anniversary with the rose garden society this year. Please join me in giving a strong heartbeat of applause to Laurence Skelton and Carol Entweiler."

Rory leaned forward and pulled the microphone stand back up onto the platform before the scattered clapping had finished. "Thank you, Mr. Brody. I'm sure we all found that presentation informative and entertaining." He wiped his brow.

Penelope shook her head. "He *really* doesn't ad lib well, does he?"

Rory folded a section of his paper over. "And now, without further ado, please welcome Isolde Woodhouse, who will award the festival prizes."

"He got *her* name right," Penelope noted.

"Isolde would have ended him if he hadn't." Esther looked around. "What happened to Iain?"

Penelope twisted around to look. Iain had been at the other end of the tent, taking payment for the already-filled cups, but now the student who had been in charge of cleaning the tables was seated on the stool by the cash box, an open textbook in her lap. Everybody who hadn't gone off to Rosa's Cantina for tacos had already settled in, so there weren't any customers.

Penelope looked outside the tent, and finally located him seated in the last row of folding chairs next to Linnea Kowalcik. "There he is." Linnea and Iain were the only two in the row.

Esther shook her head. "If they're trying to keep her husband from finding out, they need to be more discreet than that. Or maybe they're not trying to keep it a secret anymore. Look at how they're leaning toward each other."

Indeed, the anticipation of success made them careless. Linnea turned to Iain, adjusted her halter top, and licked her lips suggestively.

Penelope sighed. "I wish I could pull that off." She glanced over at Jake, who had pulled the microphone stand away from Rory and set it up on solid ground for the waiting Isolde. Her shih tzu rested in her arms, not a hair out of place. "If I tried, I'd just make us both laugh."

"Oh, please. I've seen the looks he gives you. You're doing just fine." Esther dismissed Iain and Linnea with a sniff. "The two of *you* have something with a solid foundation. Those two are building their future on a dais about as sturdy as the one that's about to collapse under Rory." She looked back at the platform again. "Or maybe burn due to faulty wiring. Are you really supposed to chain extension cords and surge protectors together like that?"

Penelope grimaced. "From the look on Jake's face when he saw it, I'd guess not."

Up in front of the platform, Isolde handed Guinevere to Rory. Penelope couldn't decide who was more horrified by this development, dog or man. But neither voiced a complaint.

Jake strode back to the beer tent, ducking under the tape to get to their table.

Penelope waited until he had sat down. "Well done on keeping all the presenters alive." She adjusted the neckline of her t-shirt and licked her lower lip. That was when she found out she had a bit of cotton candy stuck there.

Jake grinned and put one arm around her waist. "You have a stealth sexy vibe going on," he said next to her ear. "Linnea has nothing on you."

"Ah, but you *were* watching her."

"Purely professionally. I was keeping tabs on the professor for a friend."

Penelope glanced at him, but his attention was back on Isolde, who had finished announcing the prizes for best junior gardener, best smelling rose, and most colorful garden.

"And now it is time to learn who has won the coveted spot of Gardener of the Year." Isolde's already perfect posture somehow got straighter. "The judges this year faced many hardships, because there were so many lovely gardens. But also because a number of people attempted to sway the judges' choices, or circumvent the rules. I am recommending to the board that this be the last year of the competition, in this form at least."

Jake sighed. "Yes, please."

Isolde smiled. "However, the judges persevered. The points have been totaled and a winner chosen." She held up an envelope and removed a slip of paper.

Penelope watched Iain and Linnea.

"This year's Gardener of the Year, who will conduct cere-monial duties and also have the tie-breaking vote on the rose garden committee is..."

Everyone in the area leaned forward.

"Sherry Hagger. Congratulations, Sherry!"

Iain stared at Isolde in shock. Linnea frowned and looked at him. All the flirtatious behavior between the two had been wiped away, replaced by surprise and anger.

Penelope knew she'd seen that garden with Esther, but

she'd seen a lot of gardens with Esther. "Which one was Sherry's?"

"The oak with the tree swing where the child was posing. Sherry pays a rotation of children to dress up in vintage costumes and swing during the festival weekend. This year it paid off." Esther didn't sound very impressed. Grudgingly, she added, "Her roses are spectacular."

Sherry Hagger walked toward the podium. She looked every inch the gardener in her broad-brimmed hat, jeans with dirt stains on the knees, and unfashionable clogs.

Penelope remembered the child, a bored-looking girl fidgeting with the sleeves of her dress as she sat on the swing. The yard also had a fountain in the corner, a reproduction of the birth of Venus with water pooling in the clamshell base. "I take it Sherry would vote for the downtown site?" The extortion notes left for the judges would have knocked her out of the competition in two ways.

"Oh, yes. Sherry's chair of one of the downtown renewal committees. There's no way she would have funneled all that traffic to the edge of town."

Iain had left his seat and advanced on Isolde. "Let me see that." He grabbed the results envelope from her, ignoring Sherry, who was gaping at him.

Jake got up and slipped under the tape surrounding the tent.

With a scornful sniff, Isolde addressed Iain. "Mr. Hotz! We are in the middle of the ceremony. Kindly return to your seat."

Iain looked at the slip of paper, then tossed it in the air. "This was *rigged*."

Esther laughed under her breath. "Now *there's* the pot calling the kettle black."

Isolde's gaze had turned so frosty it made Penelope uncomfortable from twenty feet away. "Sit *down*, Mr. Hotz."

She turned to Sherry Hagger and smiled. "Congratulations, Sherry. You are an inspiration to us all."

Despite Isolde's attempt to keep the ceremony moving along, everyone's attention was still on Iain. Even Sherry still stared at him.

Jake stepped up to Iain and gestured to the side. Penelope had seen him do this before; with a combination of moving into someone's space and offering a sympathetic ear, Jake could deescalate a confrontation without touching anyone.

Iain took one step back, then another. The two men moved to the side of the podium, where they started an intense, whispered conversation.

Isolde's smile was looking a bit forced, but she mimed clapping as Sherry went back to her seat, and the crowd played along. "I want to thank you all for helping make this year's Rose Garden Society Festival a success. As you know, this is my last year as chairperson of the festival." She acknowledged the applause. "Thank you. I've enjoyed my time —"

At the edge of the podium, Iain's conversation with Jake suddenly got louder. "— my *house*?" His hands balled into fists.

Penelope glanced at Esther. "Uh oh." She got up from her seat.

Esther grabbed at her sleeve. "Wait, what are you doing?"

Penelope didn't have an answer to that, but she wasn't going to sit and watch while someone tried to hurt Jake. She ducked under the tape and hastened toward the two men, arriving just in time to see Iain throw a wide haymaker at Jake's chin.

Jake ducked the blow and stepped to the side.

Off balance now, Iain fell onto the podium, catching the edge on the side of his thigh. He clutched his leg and rolled.

At first Penelope thought Iain kept rolling from the pain.

Then she realized the whole podium was rocking back and forth. Still towering over Isolde at the edge of the podium, Rory Nestor swayed. He extended his arms — and Guinevere — to keep his balance. The shih tzu's eyes bulged out even more, and she yipped once.

With the sound of splintering wood, the podium collapsed to one side. Rory threw his arms up as he fell, launching Guinevere into the air.

The little dog sailed in an arc high over Isolde's head.

Two things happened then: Rory landed squarely on Iain, and Penelope jumped to the side and snatched the shih tzu from the air.

Safe in Penelope's arms, Guinevere blinked once, then licked her face. Penelope smiled at her and rubbed the dog's ears. All those years coaching her son's baseball team hadn't been a waste. She could catch a wild throw with the best of them.

y the time the paramedics arrived to look at Iain's leg and ribs, the ceremony was well and truly over.

Penelope had returned Guinevere to a thankful Isolde. The other woman had the presence of mind to return to the microphone. "Thank you." Then she walked away, Guinevere in her arms, heading toward the parking lot.

Jake had helped Rory up. The council member watched Isolde walk away, and looked to the microphone, as if remembering he was supposed to be emceeing. Then he glanced out at the sea of cell phones raised to record the event, shook his head, and walked away.

That left Iain on the podium, cursing and alternately grabbing his leg and his ribs where Rory's elbow had landed when he'd fallen. He batted Jake's hand away when Jake tried to help him up. Though she couldn't hear his words distinctly, Penelope remembered some of the language he was using from *Gravity's Rainbow*.

Jake drew back to stand next to her, wrapping an arm

around her waist. "Nice catch." He pressed a kiss to her temple.

"Almost as impressive as you breaking someone's leg without even touching him." She leaned her head against his shoulder as they watched the confusion in front of them. A firetruck slowly drove up the walkway on the other side, revolving red lights throwing odd highlights. "You'll have to teach me that technique someday."

"I don't think his leg is really broken." He laughed once. "Somehow, I don't think our English professor has been in many fights. If he telegraphed his punch like that against someone who wanted to hurt him, he'd have been in trouble."

"More fencing and less brawling at the national conferences, probably." Penelope glanced over her shoulder to make sure Esther was doing well and saw Josie sitting at the table with Puggins. "What did you say to set him off?"

"I told him there was no point in yelling at Isolde, because we'd already taken the dogs from his house. That seemed to upset him for some reason."

Of the four men on the firetruck, three were attending to Iain, and the fourth was shaking his head and unplugging the equipment from the surge protectors and extension cords. "Well, if we can't get him on dognapping or arson, maybe he'll at least end up with a fine for destroying property. That podium is toast."

Jake looked dubiously at the wreckage in front of them. "That podium should have been turned into a bonfire last year." He looked behind Penelope's head and nodded to someone. "And I don't think Iain's going to get away with everything."

Having established that Iain's neck wasn't injured, the firemen helped him off the platform onto his good leg. Detective Brianna Sanchez stepped forward, looking even tinier than usual among the bulk of the firemen. She held up her badge and appeared to be introducing herself to the professor.

Penelope looked over at her husband. "You told her what was going on."

"I... suggested that he might be a person of interest in the car fires. They had a partial print on a box of matches, but didn't get any hits in the system. She bought beer from him an hour ago and took the cup to be processed. I assume she's back because it matched." He shrugged. "This will be a good collar for her. She'll build a good case."

Iain reclined on the stretcher. He looked around the crowd, obviously searching for someone. Penelope followed his gaze and saw the empty back row. "Doesn't look like Linnea is waiting around to see what's going to happen to him." She grabbed Jake's arm. "Wait, what if she's going back to Iain's house to destroy evidence?"

"Then she's an idiot. Sanchez will have sent uniforms over to his house to secure the scene the minute the print match came back. The car fires were making the chief look bad. They have more than enough resources for the case."

Penelope relaxed. "As long as someone takes care of Barnaby." After all, it wasn't the dog's fault his owner was such a terrible human being.

The paramedics wheeled the stretcher toward the ambulance waiting in the parking lot, Detective Sanchez walking alongside. The staff photographer for the town newspaper knelt to get shots of the scene.

Penelope and Jake ducked back under the tape into the beer tent and sat down at their table again. Josie was showing Esther pictures on her phone and pointing out the differences between the fursuits.

Two women sat down at the table behind them. Penelope remembered seeing them at a house she and Esther had viewed over the weekend. "The judges must be blind.

Everyone knows Sherry brought in a professional consultant," the first one said.

The second snorted. "And the plants! Not a native in the lot."

"Hmph. At least she doesn't spray pesticides all over the place." The first woman shook her head. "Next year. If we can just figure out who is doing the judging, I think we have a shot."

Jake met Penelope's gaze. "I'm beginning to think all gardeners are crazy. I'm done."

"Only after you plant my pomegranate tree." She looked around and noted how many people were leaving the area. "Do you have your drill in the car?"

"Yes, why?" He looked toward the booths, which were deserted. "Don't tell me. Tamsin and Leo were responsible for recruiting people to disassemble everything as well."

Esther looked up from her perusal of fluffy tails. "I'll start calling people and see who I can get to help."

CHAPTER 30

Muscles aching and still full of the pepperoni pizza Esther had ordered to feed the small band of volunteers dismantling the booths, Penelope burst through the front door triumphantly. She held up her lock picks. "I did it!" She leaned against the door to close it and looked at her phone. "And it only took me... ninety-two minutes."

Jake tilted his head to see her without getting up from the couch. "Congratulations!"

Brutus lifted his head from his spot on Jake's lap, decided she didn't look like she was going to give him any treats, and dropped his head down again.

"I mean, at this rate, someone could throw a rock through the window, pack up all our belongings, and load them into a truck before I got the first door unlocked, but I'll get there." Penelope carefully zipped up her lock pick set and stowed it in her backpack.

Jake nodded. "I have every faith you'll become a more efficient criminal soon." He shoved the dog off him to make room for her on the couch. "But I'm impressed anyhow.

That's not an easy lock."

Snuggling up against him, Penelope patted his leg. "It helped that someone sprayed it with graphite recently."

"Ah. Well." He winced and looked at her. "That just makes it a little easier. It's not cheating."

"I'm not complaining. If it stuck like it normally does, I'd have been out there all night." She rested her head against his shoulder. "Now I have all this free time I wasn't planning on."

"Really." He stopped with his wine glass halfway to his mouth.

"Yeah. I guess I could just get some extra rest."

"That would be the responsible thing to do." He sipped his wine. "Or…"

"Oh, right, I guess I could look through the gardening catalogs and pick out a pomegranate tree."

"Definitely a possibility." He finished his wine and set down his glass. "Or…"

"Or I guess we could go celebrate the conclusion of your first successful case as a private investigator."

"*Our* first case."

Penelope stood up, took his hand, and drew him to his feet. "I even made a soundtrack for the occasion." She pulled out her phone and tapped the screen. The horns and guitar riff of the original *Magnum, P.I.* theme song played.

Jake groaned. "I've created a monster."

Penelope grinned. "You lock up the house and I'll take care of the dog." She danced toward the freezer where they kept food stuffed toys to keep Brutus occupied, the music still coming from her phone. "But hurry up. I drew the line at the *Hart to Hart* music, so the soundtrack isn't that long."

Jake's burst of laughter nearly drowned out the phone. "I can't wait to find out what made the cut."

Penelope smiled as she danced up the stairs.

* * *

I HOPE YOU ENJOYED READING THIS INSTALLMENT OF *THE Penelope Standing Mysteries!*

If you would like to be notified when the next book is available, as well as receive exclusive short stories, you can sign up for my free newsletter at https://tmbaumgartner.com/subscribe/.

ACKNOWLEDGMENTS

As always, my friends and family have helped me with this book by just being there. Extra kudos to Hilary, who read the beta version of this manuscript and told me she was ready to die for Smaug Orson, and Brutus was right to pee on the pug.

My brother Eric continues to try to tell me what to do, but at least in this case it's because I asked him to proofread the book. Apparently, my just-barely-nodding acquaintance with English grammar causes him grief. I consider it payback for having to deal with all the teachers who winced when they recognized my last name.

(I'm pretty sure the teachers had rock-paper-scissors contests every year to determine who got stuck with me, and that's not all Eric's fault since I was the fourth kid. But Eric certainly did his share.)